DIFFUSION

The Spectrum Series

SAMANTHA MINA

DIFFUSION

BOOK 2 OF A SERIES

For Katie Geary Miller
who helped me fall in love with Second Earth
all over again.

PRONUNCIATION GUIDE

Acci: *"AX-ee"*
Arrhyth: *"AR-hith"*
Buird: *"Bird"*
Ichthyosis: *"Ik-thee-OH-sis"*
Leavesleft: *"LEEV-ssleft"*
Lechatelierite: *"Luh-shaht-LEER-ahyt"*
(rhymes with "light")
Nuria: *"NER-ee-ah"*
Qui Tsop: *"Key Sop"*

NORTHWESTERN HEMISPHERE OF SECOND EARTH

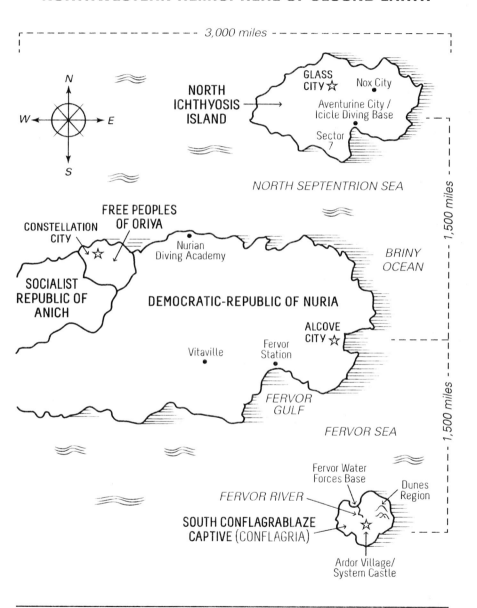

PART I
THE CIVIL WAR

...Then, like a swollen river that has broken bank and wall,
The human flood came pouring with the red flags over all,
And kindled eyes all blazing bright with revolution's heat,
And flashing swords reflecting rigid faces in the street.
Pouring on, pouring on,
To a drum's loud threatening beat,
And the war-hymns and the cheering of the people in the street.

And so it must be while the world goes rolling round its course,
The warning pen shall write in vain, the warning voice grow hoarse,
But not until a city feels Red Revolution's feet
Shall its sad people miss awhile the terrors of the street
The dreadful everlasting strife
For scarcely clothes and meat
In that pent track of living death the city's cruel street.

——*"Faces in the Street" by Henry Lawson*

AMBREK COPPERTUS

Her neck snapped with the impact of his kick and she dropped like a stone to the hardwood floor. Blood sprayed from her broken body onto his white suit. She lay, lifeless and bleeding, a grotesque, red doll beneath his silver-grey stare. Without a second thought, he turned his back on her and ran into the night.

That was the story of my sister, System Water Forces Commander Crimson Cerise, and the one who took her life, Ichthyothian Diving Admiral Cease Lechatelierite. I saw everything in visions. Roughly five months ago, on July twenty-fifth of the ninety-third age of Second Earth's seventh era, Lechatelierite killed my sister while in his own POW cell. He didn't do it cleanly, either, with Nordic technology. He broke her in half with his boot.

Preceding Crimson, Scarlet July was his first victim. He killed her too, but not in body. He corrupted her mind, turned her into a tool of the Ichthyothians, into a radical revolutionary, into the villain responsible for depriving Conflagria from the spectrum it needed to survive and prosper.

Before Scarlet was deported in the eighty-seventh age, she lived right across the Dust Path from my family, in Ardor Village of the South Conflagrablaze Captive. She was timid, rarely leaving her parent's home, except to go swimming in the Fervor River. The few times I spotted her outside, I noticed how the light played upon her fiery, red hair and how her emerald-green eyes sparkled when she miraculously stared at the sun. I found myself strangely drawn to her cautious demeanor, outlandish appearance and peculiar magic. She was beautiful to my fourteen-age-old eyes. I was glad the System betrothed her to me. I furtively admired her from afar, awaiting the day we'd be old enough to be together, the day I could finally remove the shades of self-doubt from her eyes and help her see how amazing she really was. And, she'd adore me with all her heart and tell me every day that she owed her happiness all to me. This was the fantasy that filled my adolescent days.

And then, she was deported.

In a moment, my dream shattered like the weak shell of a premature scabrous-dragon. The System didn't assign me a new wife, either; I was told to wait indefinitely for a woman to get widowed early. Betrothals were made at birth or early childhood at the latest, and everyone within a ten-age bracket of me was already taken. But, that hardly mattered to me anyway, because I didn't want anyone else. I wanted Scarlet.

Six ages passed. My family was one of the privileged few to know of the secret Ichthyo-Conflagrian War, since my sister was chosen for the Water Forces at a very young age. So, five months ago, on July thirty-first of the ninety-third age, when the Fire Pit literally exploded, I immediately knew the Ichthyothians were responsible. I wondered, how did they destroy the Core Crystal without magic? The System's finest spectroscopers believed the Crystal was impervious to Nordic weaponry. Only powerful magic could harm it, and the spectral-thought-direction made it unlikely any mage would ever want to. Moreover, even if someone wanted to, they wouldn't be strong enough to make a dent in it.

Or, so we thought.

I remembered every minute of that fateful July day. I remembered standing at the end of the line surrounding the Pit, awaiting my daily fire ration. I remembered the boom of the Crystal's detonation and the earthquake that followed. I remembered how the daylight abruptly darkened to night, as Conflagria visually adjusted to the Earth's thirty-six-hour rotation.

And, then, there was the diffusion. I'd never experienced anything quite like it. My body felt as though fully submerged in ice-water. Flashes of amber and copper bled from my every pore. My hands and feet went numb and blood drained from my face. My weakened fingers dropped my empty torch. My ears could hardly register the screams all around me. Dizzy and shivering, I fought to stay conscious.

Only a few dozen yards in front of me, a small, black-robed figure barreled out of the Pit's narrow stairwell. As he ran, his hood flew back, revealing a pale, sharp-featured face, steely eyes and a wild mop of shiny, dark hair. I'd seen that face countless times in my nightmarish visions. It was him. My sister's killer. While every mage in the System knew and feared the name of Cease Lechatelierite, few had ever seen his face and lived to tell of it.

In his arms lay the tiny, unconscious form of a rosy-cheeked, red-haired girl in a blood-red robe. Even at a distance and even after six ages, I still recognized her. My exiled betrothed, Scarlet July.

Shocked, I just stood there and gawked as Lechatelierite plowed through the crowd, heading my way. Though I was probably twice his size, I was the one knocked to the sand when he slammed into me. He leapt right over my supine frame and kept running.

Seconds later, an Ichthyothian carrier dashed across the deep-brown sky like an elephantine manta-ray. It poured magicless fire into the empty Pit, swooped over to Lechat-elierite and dropped a ladder. Hoisting Scarlet's limp form over his shoulder, he scrambled up the rungs. With a roar, the craft rocketed into the northern horizon.

My chest trembled as I slowly got to my feet. How and why was Scarlet July here, in Conflagria? Why was she in the Fire Pit while it was under attack? Why was *he* taking her aboard their carrier? Was she a prisoner of the enemy? Nothing made sense.

I didn't have to wait long for answers. No, Scarlet wasn't a prisoner of the Ichthyothians. She was one of them. She'd reached into the Pit with her own hair and destroyed the very sustenance of her people.

At once, the island cleaved in two. Half the population saw Scarlet July as their liberator. As they learned of the 'mind-control' that 'oppressed' Conflagria for eras, they declared their intent to revolt against the System. Scarlet July was called home, to be their revolutionary leader.

The other half of the population saw her for what she truly was—a tool of the Ichthyothian enemy and the heinous thief of our magical powers. We were handicapped without spectrum. Without the Crystal, we were blind, deaf and lame. Now, Conflagria had neither magic nor technology. Compared to the rest of Second Earth, we were helpless and primitive. Until Scarlet diffused the spectral web, the System was leading Conflagria into a victorious war against Ichthyosis, on its way to achieve greatness in the world, on its way to build a powerful empire that'd stretch both north and south. Scarlet took away the hope of her nation to rise above obscurity and emerge as a superpower in the international arena. Scarlet transformed Conflagria into a third-world country, ravaged by civil war.

The day Scarlet returned to Conflagria as the 'Red Leader'—August seventh—I swore on my sister's grave I'd destroy her and her puppet-master.

"Crimson Cerise," I cried as I sat by her grave that night, "I promise I'll avenge your death and defend the System for which you gave your life." I grasped a withering, red sandflower by her tombstone. "I'll kill that Ichthyothian tool, Scarlet July, and the one who corrupted her and took you away from me, Cease Lechatelierite," I spat his ugly, Nordic name. It sounded like a mouthful of broken glass. I crushed the flower in my large hands, scattering petal shreds over my sister's engraved name. "Your brother won't let you down."

SCARLET JULY

Shivering, I pulled my robe tighter around my body. I rolled over in my straw tarp, facing the rough, wooden wall of the old, abandoned cabin that now served as the stronghold of the three revolutionary leaders. It was midnight on the twenty-second of December—the winter solstice and the coldest day of the Conflagrian winter, thus far. It was one-hundred degrees.

After five ages in Nuria and a couple months in Ichthyosis, one would think I'd be able to handle a hundred-degree day without a chill. But, I'd braved Alcove City and Aventurine City with an aura. Spectrum coursed through my veins, warm and revitalizing.

Now, however, I was completely on my own. I was no longer the Multi-Source Enchant. I wasn't a mage, at all. I was nothing but a sixteen-age-old girl who stood less than five feet tall. My red hair hung limply and lifelessly on my shoulders and my eyes were too weak to even glance at the orange, Conflagrian sun. But, I was still a war veteran and the leader of the first Conflagrian rebellion. Magical or not, I was determined to fulfill my duty to my people.

But, thankfully, I wasn't doing it alone. I had two, fearless co-leaders. Through fire and ice, thick and thin, I had my childhood friend, Fair Gabardine, and my old neighbor, Ambrek Coppertus, walking with me on the arduous path to freedom. My experience in the Nurro-Ichthyothian

Diving Fleet, Fair's experience in the System Water Forces and Ambrek's rather extensive inside knowledge of the System, all intertwined beautifully into a tapestry of resistance. Since August, the three of us were mobilizing the disgruntled masses against the System. Named after me, their leader, we became known as the Reds. This was the Red Revolution.

It may sound glorious, to be a civil war warrior. But, honestly, it was nothing but dirty work. Day and night, it was a struggle to survive, let alone keep the cause alive and battle the opposition. Yes, I truly believed this was my life's purpose, the reason I was born. But, honestly, I hated every minute of it. I was good at pretending to be alright in front of everyone, but in the dark of night, the real Scarlet July emerged. The real Scarlet was exhausted, physically and emotionally. The real Scarlet was lonely, tired and afraid of the future. Participating in two wars in the course of fifteen months had eroded my passion. And, I could no longer turn to magic for physical relief or replenishment. How did the Nordic soldiers do it? How could they continue fighting for ages upon ages, without a single photon of spectrum? After months of bending, I was about to break.

I was certainly no Cease Lechatelierite.

I turned over, tarp creaking. Why did my thoughts always circle back to Cease Lechatelierite? I swallowed. Without spectrum, my memory was far from perfect, but I still remembered verbatim what Fair said as we left Ichthyosis on August seventh: 'If his memory makes you happy, then by all means, go ahead and love him.' Well, she was wrong. His memory didn't make me happy, it made me miserable. And, as a warrior, I didn't have the luxury of letting that misery show. I had to stay strong for my people. I had to keep all thoughts of Cease bottled up along with that of my family and the countless soldiers—Nordic and

Conflagrian alike—whom I lost, since my military career began. No, Cease wasn't dead. But, he was three-thousand miles away, on the ice island to which I could never return.

The worst part was, now that my aura diffused and took my eidetic memory with it, I was already beginning to forget the conversations we had, or the many textures of his throat-mage-like voice, or how his face looked when he smiled at me for the first and only time. Memories were all I'd ever have of Cease, and I was losing even those. The more time passed, the more they slipped from my mind like sand between fingers.

I did remember that today, December twenty-second, was Cease's eighteenth birthday. I also knew this day would pass like any other for him, as all holidays and special occasions were ignored in the Nordic military. I was probably the only one on Second Earth who thought of it. But, I didn't want to think about him anymore. I told myself every day that I had to move on.

Sometimes, I felt angry at him for what happened on August seventh. It was difficult enough to part in the first place—why did he have to kiss me over and over and tell me he loved me? It was pointless to bind me to him like that when he knew we'd never see each other again. I would've been perfectly content with a short embrace and a simple 'good-bye,' but he just *had* to go and complicate everything and make me love him more.

Tears streamed into the ragged wad I was using for a pillow. Fair usually shared my room, but tonight she was visiting Seventh Cabin to see her new 'friend,' Prunus Persica. Ambrek was still around, though. He was in the adjoining room. So, I had to stifle my sobs. Because soldiers didn't cry.

AMBREK COPPERTUS

I couldn't sleep. Even after five months, I was yet to adapt to the thirty-six hour days. Twenty-four were enough, for Tincture's sake.

I heard a faint gasp through the wooden wall. So, Scarlet was crying, again. Shocker. In the light of day, she always put on a brave face. But, I knew the array of emotions that plagued her sleepless nights. Grief. Longing. Confusion. Despair. I knew all the Red Leader's weaknesses—or, as the First Earthlings would say, her 'Achilles heel.' I knew where to strike, when the time was right. And, without her, the revolution would crumble, no doubt.

But, the time wasn't right, yet. It'd only been five months. The System wasn't done using her.

I was the thorn in the side of the Red Revolution. The invisible crack in the castle of glass. In August, when Scarlet came home, the System gave me, her old neighbor, a unique assignment: get close to her. Win her trust and respect. Become a double agent. Report back to the System with intel straight from the mouth of our greatest threat. And, I did it. Now, I was none other than the Red Co-Leader, alongside Scarlet's hotheaded best friend, Fair Gabardine.

All the great military and political leaders in First Earth history knew to keep some secrets, especially during times of war. But, Scarlet, being young and naïve, kept no such reserves. She didn't dare move a muscle without consulting Fair and I first.

She treated me as though I were Lechatelierite.

It took me until November to realize it, but now it seemed obvious. I wasn't particularly stern or domineering, yet she was obedient to me. I wasn't her commander—quite the opposite, in fact—yet, she religiously awaited my approval before carrying out any plan. I didn't act distant or aloof from her, yet she often addressed me with caution. She even called me 'sir' sometimes, though the Reds certainly weren't a formal military operation like the System Water Forces or the Ichthyothian Diving Fleet. It was like obsequiousness to Lechatelierite was so deeply rooted in her psyche, her subconscious needed me to fill his absence. It was like her mind required his overbearing presence to function properly. The damage her ex-commander inflicted on her mental health was glaringly apparent to me, every time we interacted. Day after day, her behavior served to remind me of how he corrupted her.

I should've been glad Scarlet was falling apart, because she was my enemy. But, a small part of me still cared for her—the part that clung to my youthful dreams. My fourteen and twenty-age-old selves warred daily. I had to remind myself constantly I had a patriotic duty to fulfill and a sister to avenge. I had to tell myself, day and night, it was pointless to waste emotional energy on a person who was gone forever.

The real Scarlet July died the day she enlisted in Cease Lechatelierite's fleet.

CEASE LECHATELIERITE

A blur of grey shot to my left, mere inches from my elbow, descending sharply into the cobalt-blue depths of the North Septentrion Sea.

I breathed out through my nostrils. "Dammit, Buird, I've told you several times to widen your circumference!"

"Yes, sir!" Inexor's flustered voice replied.

Surface-riding on Nurtic Leavesleft's crystalline, I looked over my shoulder at the string of twenty, nervous Nurian trainees, clinging to the handlebars.

"Alright, men, this move is called 'jackknife.'" I got into position. "Begin by straightening your back and hooking your feet on the rungs. Then, twist your hips around, like so." I tumbled neatly off the side of the shuttle. "Now, it's your turn. Three…two…one…launch! Arms above your head. Good. Now, bend your elbows for impact. You should reach Buird…now!"

Twenty pairs of hands groped for the handlebars, but Inexor came in too steep and everyone wound up splatting against his hull like insects.

"During combat, crystallines won't always be able to maintain consistent patterns or pre-determined series of formations," I growled, stationed at the tail. "Buird was only a handful of degrees off; you must adapt!" I glared at their tinted visors. The old helmets had clear glass. It was strange not to see their eyes anymore.

I glanced at the sleeve of my diving suit. Time to wrap up this spectacle. "All shuttles dock. All hands to the lecture hall."

"Ugh, sir, can't we at least shower first?" piped Arrhyth Link, the sub-leader of unit eleven. Link's head got a bit inflated since he played a small role in the infiltration, last July—back-up getaway pilot. He was a good pilot, thanks in large part to Leavesleft's after-hours instruction, but no amount of skill gave anybody the right to be mouthy with me.

"Are you questioning me, soldier?" I barked.

"No, sir." His voice went small.

"Your performance today doesn't kindle my sympathy," I shot.

"I'm sorry, sir."

We rode back to base in silence. With a tight chest, I thought about the twenty-five, even greener Nurians arriving tomorrow.

Turned out, ending the Core Crystal didn't end the Ich-thyo-Conflagrian War. Within a few weeks since the diffusion of the spectral web, the supporters of the System regrouped and, against all odds, found a way to wage war again. With neither magic nor technology of their own—armed only with their creativity and resourcefulness—they managed to put up a surprisingly strong fight. Though still ignorant of the relatively new Nurro-Ichthyothian Alliance, the System risked angering 'neutral' Nuria by stealing crafts and supplies from the Fervor Gulf ports, to use against us. With plenty of ships and a handful of diving suits to dissect, it was only a matter of time before they'd figure out how to construct their own.

The Nurian members of the Alliance Committee were in uproar. They said, if I didn't find a way put an end to the Conflagrians' theft ASAP, Nuria would 'remove itself from the conflict.' As if that weren't bad enough, both nations were also furious at me for declaring victory five months ago, then returning to battle in a matter of weeks. Every day, my name was thrown around the media—I heard everything from 'the great and victorious Admiral Lechatelierite' to 'the lying scoundrel who can't live up to his own name and cease this ridiculous, international affair.' I was under growing amounts of pressure from all sides to make the fighting miraculously stop. Nuria was allowing virtually anyone into their military academies now, graduating dozens on a weekly basis, thinking that'd accelerate the war effort. They didn't know they were just overwhelming me with a ridiculously large, unskilled fleet. Currently, there were several hundred divers—only a handful of them Ichthyothian—living at Icicle. Before the alliance was formed, one-hundred-ten was the largest fleet I ever led. In my opinion, barely a quarter of my soldiers were competent enough for real combat. Our casualty rate almost equaled the Diving Academy graduation rate. Every day we went out to sea, dozens of souls were added to my conscious. Yes, my conscious actually picked up on that sort of thing.

Or, it did for a time. Allow me to backtrack a bit.

Scarlet departed on August seventh, leaving me shaken up and confused out of my mind. All quiet on the battlefront, my personal crisis flew under the radar for the remainder of the summer. But, by September, the war heated back up, big time. Thrown into combat on a near-daily basis, I spent that whole month sick—headaches, nausea, vomiting, night-sweats, tremors, you name it—because, for the first time in my life, I saw myself as a monster with bloodstained hands. I was frightened and appalled by my own brutality. And, as my performance deteriorated, more newbies dropped like sleet. Which made me even more upset. It was a vicious spiral.

By October, I realized I needed to be my old self—my *real* self—again. I had to be. I knew the lifestyle of the

Leader of the Ichthyothian Resistance couldn't accommodate such hypersensitivity. I had to re-callous myself. I wondered, how did Scarlet—compassionate, sweet Scarlet—carry on, day after day, without crumbling? How did she do so well as my second commander, not only watching her Nordic comrades die but actively killing mages, her own people? How was she serving at the forefront of the Red Revolution now, commanding armies of Conflagrians against one another? How did she make it so far with such a soft, emotional interior? Because my 'new self' sure wasn't sustainable. I definitely couldn't spend the rest of my life reacting to everything, not if I was going survive an international war. I was certainly no Scarlet July.

So, as October and November came and went, I slowly killed my heart. It wasn't easy. I reread hundreds of pages of old, psych material from my days in the Childhood Program and received private counsel from Colonel Autoero Austere. And, slowly but surely, battles became easier to wage. I stopped throwing up and having nightmares. I felt stronger and more in control of myself. In the wake of casualty, I found myself caring less for the individual lives lost and more for what those deaths meant for the greater, Nurro-Ichthyothian Resistance. Instead of grieving and self-flagellating, I'd pick myself up, pull myself together, learn my lesson and strategize ways to get the job done with less casualties next time.

Yet, even as I grew numb to the world, there was still one wound I couldn't close. There was one fire I couldn't stomp out. One thing that distinguished me from my old, stoic self. One facet of the weaker Cease that remained. My attachment to Scarlet. My pointless, stupid, painful, self-destructive attachment to a person living three-thousand miles away whom I knew I'd never see again. And, as Conflagria was both secluded and void of technology, I had no way of

communicating with her. Not knowing how she was doing—
or, who she was with—drove me crazy, every day.

"Your performance today was completely unacceptable,"
I grumbled now, as my soldiers poured into the lecture hall,
soaked and exhausted. I launched into a three-hour critique of the day's practice and didn't dismiss them until a
full hour after dinner should've been.

"Second Commander, report!" I called as the hall emptied.

Inexor Buird was my best friend before he got captured
by the System in the summer of the ninety-second age.
Since his return, our friendship sailed on rough seas. He
was furious over how I treated Fair Gabardine, whom
he apparently grew to care for during his imprisonment.
Things between us briefly improved when I told him how
sorry I was for harming her and how many times I tried to
apologize to her. But, the tension revived when he peeked
at my logs from the months he was MIA and learned exactly what went down in the Fire Pit during the infiltration.
He grew suspicious I broke the Laws of Emotional Protection. And, of course, he was right. I didn't behave logically
during that mission; I allowed my feelings for Scarlet to
impact the decisions I made and the risks I was willing to
take. He confronted me about it and got real pissed when I
admitted I loved Scarlet and was pretty sure she loved me,
too. So, I called him a hypocrite, since he himself broke the
same laws, for an enemy soldier, no less.

As for his performance in the sea, that didn't normalize,
either. Before Scarlet came along, Inexor was the best
soldier I had. But, now, he might as well be Apha Edenta.
Maybe it was because he was still recouping from his long
imprisonment. Maybe it was because he couldn't bear to
serve the man who hurt the woman he claimed to love.
Maybe he was just out of practice, having spent eleven

months rotting in a cell. Whatever it was, I didn't care anymore. I just wanted a competent co-commander.

"What the hell is wrong with you, soldier?" I demanded, looking him in the eye. "Your sloppiness today could've killed someone!"

Inexor was silent.

"I asked you a question!"

His cool blue eyes passed over my head. "I'm sorry, Cease."

"It's 'Admiral, sir'!"

He blinked. "I'll work harder, okay? Calm down. You're always so strung-up."

I took a step forward. "If I'm strung-up, it's because of incompetents like you! Compared to your predecessor—"

"Oh, so *that's* what this is all about!" Inexor roared. "You'd prefer my *predecessor* over me, is that right, Mr. Admiral, sir? Never mind that she turned traitor in the Fire Pit last July and tried to kill you, or that her spectral twining leaked intel to the System, or that she lied her ass off just to get here in the first place, or that the truth of her origin caused near-mutiny. Forget all that; *she's* still the second commander you want, not me!" He dug his hands into his pockets. "Never mind that I was locked up for nearly an age because I saved your neck. Never mind that the reason that battle got shot to hell in the first place was because you were too cocky to listen to *my* warnings about the Underwater Fire!"

"Silence!" I erupted. "We're not discussing personal matters, here; this discussion is about your circus act in the sea!"

"Personal matters?" Inexor threw his arms up. "Would you call it a personal matter if Scarlet fell into the Fire Pit, during the infiltration? The spectrum would've diffused just the same, but you were willing to trash the entire war to save her life—is that just a little personal problem, Admiral, or are your screwed-up priorities a matter of national security?"

I was silent.

"Yes, technically, we both violated the Laws of Emotional Protection," he went on. "But, unlike you, my 'violation' was all in my head. I didn't act on it and I certainly didn't endanger my country for it."

I folded my arms. The only reason he didn't 'act' on it was because Fair didn't let him. "Are you actually worried about national security, or is this about Fair Gabardine?" I growled. "Because you're jealous Scarlet reciprocated my feelings while Fair never gave a dragon turd for you?"

Inexor looked slapped. I knew I crossed a line, but I didn't care.

"You want to talk about Fair?" Inexor squared his jaw. "Okay, let's talk about her. Let's talk about how you shot the Geneva Convention to hell, torturing her. The way you interrogated her—it was abuse. Criminal." He paused, cobalt eyes enraged. I guessed he didn't really forgive me for that, after all. "There's no other way to put it, Cease: you committed a felony. And, if the Alliance Committee ever got wind of it, you wouldn't be here anymore. You'd be behind bars."

His heated words hung in the icy air. And, without dismissal, Inexor turned on his heel and stalked out the door.

SCARLET JULY

The door creaked. Instinctively, I leapt to my feet and wiped my face with my sleeve.

"Why are you standing?" Ambrek came in, amber-gold eyes wide. As usual, his copper hair stood on end, as though oiled with dragon fat. Before the spectral web diffused, he was a hand mage and an Iridescent—he had one source, but two colored frequencies.

"What do you want, sir?" I asked, sitting down heavily.

"'Sir'?" Ambrek sat beside me, gathering the folds of his copper-green robe. "I'm just checking on my friend. Are you okay?"

"Yes, of course."

Ambrek scooted behind me and put his hands on my tense shoulders. Giving random back massages was one of his old, hand-mage habits.

"Of course, nothing. Fair and I have been worried about you."

Heat rose to my face. "And, why's that? My performance on the battlefield hasn't—"

"Your performance on the battlefield isn't why I'm here. I didn't come into your room, in the middle of the night, to talk business. I'm not concerned about the Red Leader; I'm worried about Scarlet, the sixteen-age-old girl who cries all the time about Tincture knows what. The girl who barely eats or sleeps or discusses anything but war." He ran his hands up and down my spine.

I thought my façade was foolproof, but Ambrek saw through it, after all. "My personal junk hasn't affected the operations of our infantry. Why do you care?"

Ambrek squeezed my shoulders a little too tightly. "Since when is the revolution the only thing I care about? You don't think I care about *you?*"

"I-I'm sorry."

"And, why are you apologizing, now? Why are you always so afraid of me?"

Ambrek knelt before me on the floor, touched my chin with his fingertips and tilted my head up, forcing me to meet his gaze. The gesture reminded me so much of Cease, my eyes watered, all over again.

"This is what I mean," he murmured. "Scarlet, I understand if you miss him. Believe me, I get it. I miss my sister, every day. But, really, it's almost the new age—it's time to move on. You need to help yourself; you need to try not to think about him. Because it's destroying you. And, it's destroying our friendship. From the way you've been treating me, I think it's reasonable to assume you've been projecting your relationship with *him* on *me*. It's like your mind's been using me to compensate for his absence. I mean, you're always so cautious and apologetic toward me," he folded his arms, "and you constantly accuse me of being single-minded about the war, which I'm not. Scarlet, I'm not sure we even have a real friendship because you always treat me like I'm someone else. I think his memory is… I don't know, messing with your head, or something."

There was a tense silence. Ambrek's last line hit me like a slab of ice in the skull.

"Messing with my head?" I echoed. "You think I'm going crazy?"

"No, that's not what I meant—"

"You think I'm too weak to deal with my past? I watched my family die, for Tincture's sake, I escaped execution and survived on the Nurian streets for five ages as a *kid*. And, you think I'm going mad because I dare to shed a tear or two in middle of the night when no one's around?" I jumped to my feet, but I was still shorter than Ambrek on his knees. "I fought in the best military in the world—I was second-in-*command*—and you don't think I can cope with my own memories?"

"No, Scarlet, that's not what I meant! All I'm trying to say is, it's been like five months since you came home and it's time to leave the past in the past, or at least try to." He stood up and walked to the door. "Once you step out of his shadow and open your eyes, maybe you'll start to realize there are people *right here* who care about you and want to be there for you, no matter what. People who love you."

And, with that, the door snapped shut. I sat down and stared at the floor for a long, long time.

CEASE LECHATELIERITE

Ten men sat before me at the long table. They all wore dark suits and multicolored ties and the Nurians among them clutched large mugs of coffee. Coffee. I couldn't imagine ingesting something hot, especially in an over-heated room. It was, what, seventy degrees in here? I watched as they dropped white 'sugar' cubes into their cups. The Nurians in my fleet liked to talk about sugar, about how they missed it and wished Icicle had some. Like my fellow Ichthyothian comrades, I believed the purpose of food was nourishment, not amusement. The idea of eating for fun—consuming something just because it tasted good, even if it were unhealthy—was nuts.

I was currently visiting the Nurian Academy for a conference with the Alliance Committee. Since the summer, the relationship between the Democratic-Republic of Nuria and the North Ichthyosis Island rapidly deteriorated. This meeting was our last chance to patch up our differences before the alliance fell apart.

I was here as the sole representative of the Nurro-Ichthyothian Military—the lone white uniform in a sea of black and charcoal business suits. I didn't understand why the Trilateral Committee Chiefs—Commodore Rettahs Krad Slous and Admiral Oppre Is Sive—didn't bother to grace us with their presence today, but I was actually relieved to be free of their oversight. I never did see eye-to-eye with the Trilateral Committee.

At one end of the table was the Ichthyothian Prime Minister Rime Gelid Ascet, sipping ice-water. At the other end sat the Nurian President Georgen Winster Briggesh, nursing a frothy 'cappuccino.' Alliance Chairman Cartel Aliquot Juncture was without drink, sitting right across from me, in the center of the group. He fingered his gavel, nervous eyes darting between the two heads of state.

"Conflagria has neither magic nor technology," the Nurian President said. "Since their spectral web diffused, the System has been raiding our ports for supplies and ships to use against your nation. Nuria's economy has only recessed since becoming your ally. We can't afford to be ransacked by your enemies any longer."

To use against *your* nation. Ransacked by *your* enemies. Sweat trickled down my forehead and into my eyes, but I didn't blink. Ichthyosis's opponents were supposed to be Nuria's, too.

"Ichthyosis apologizes," Prime Minister Ascet responded. "Admiral Cease Lechatelierite of the Diving Fleet is committed to bringing the war to a close as quickly as possible."

Well, I hadn't a clue how exactly I was supposed to do that without getting directly involved in the Red Revolution—something the Alliance and Trilateral Committees strictly forbade me to do, since the millisecond the Red uprising began.

Briggesh's beady eyes raked my face. "Nuria anticipates your efforts, Admiral."

I didn't answer.

"Onto the next topic: the state of the Conflagrian Civil War," Juncture said, tapping his gavel. "The so-called 'Red Revolution' against the System is not faring well. They claim to be in desperate need of materiel. One of their leaders, Fair Antiquartz Gabardine, sent a letter appealing to the alliance for aid."

"Denied," Briggesh responded immediately, like he had the right to speak for the entire alliance.

"Mr. President," I interjected. At this, Briggesh made a big show of surprise, jolting his mug and blinking rapidly at me, as though the Leader of the Nurro-Ichthyothian Resistance wasn't expected to open his mouth at a state-of-the-war conference. "I propose a vote."

There was a pregnant pause.

"Very well, Admiral." He clasped his hands and nodded at Juncture.

"A simple majority will be taken," Juncture directed. "All in favor of complying with Gabardine's request?"

"Aye!" I exclaimed. I was the only one. I looked around, in disbelief. "You want me to accelerate the war effort. That means we can't just sit back and watch the System squash the revolution. How can we end the war without equipping our friends against the enemy?"

"The real question is, Admiral, how can we be sure these 'Reds' truly are friends of the alliance?" the Prime Minister asked.

Seriously? "We have a common enemy, sir, a shared goal: the annihilation of the System. The enemy of my enemy is my friend."

"Ah, but it's not that simple. Common enemy or not, they are still Conflagrian, which means they are of a deceitful disposition."

Blood pounded in my ears like a semi-automatic. What kind of logic was that? Who was he, to casually write off all magekind? I trusted Scarlet with my life.

"With all due respect, sir, five months ago, the Core Crystal was destroyed *by a Conflagrian*—the very individual at the forefront of the Red Revolution today. If we could trust her with the most important operation in our war to date, we can surely give her and her men some guns and ammo."

A wave of shocked murmurs swept across the room. The Trilateral Committee considered Scarlet the biggest scandal of the Ichthyothian military world, and I was aware they wanted to keep her service in the fleet hushed up. But, I figured that meant, hushed up from the media and the general public. Not from the governments of the allied nations. And, certainly not from the Ichthyothian Prime Minister or the Nurian President. The Trilateral Committee was going to have my head, once they found out about my loose lips.

That was, if the men here didn't kill me first.

"Excuse me, Admiral?" Ascet bellowed over the buzz. "We were under the impression the Diving Fleet is responsible for the diffusion."

"We are, sir." I had no choice but to spill all the gory details, now. "I allowed a Conflagrian to serve in my fleet. She was my second-in-command."

It was as though I threw a torch of spectral fire onto the table.

"Excuse me?"

"Breach of protocol!"

"Adult enlistments were open strictly to Nurian citizens!"

"Sheer recklessness!"

"This is what we get for putting a *child* in command of our troops!"

"How dare you jeopardize the entire alliance by allowing one of *them*—one of the *enemy race*—to serve!"

I was seeing red. "We can't make blanket statements like 'enemy race'!" my voice sliced into the hubbub. "I daresay, my former Second, Scarlet July, has done more for Ichthyosis than any soldier in Nordic military history. And, she's

now leading a revolution against *our* enemy—the System."
A wave of dizziness suddenly struck me. I knew this was
Nuria and all, but it was also December—why was it so
hot in here? I wiped my forehead with a napkin. "The out-
comes of the Ichthyo-Conflagrian War and the Conflagrian Civil War are inextricable. If the Reds triumph, the
System won't have the bandwidth to fight us anymore and
the international war will come to an end, once and for all."

"You would understand, Admiral, if we no longer trust
your judgment as to what would or wouldn't end the war,"
the President said. His words were backed by nine nodding
heads. "Your previous assessment was faulty indeed. Ending the Crystal last July didn't solve anything."

It didn't end the war for good, but I thought it a stretch to
claim it didn't solve *anything*. It certainly weakened the System and bought us time. Perhaps everyone forgot just how
bad things were, before the diffusion. If Scarlet didn't destroy
the Crystal, the alliance would've been crushed, by now.

But, before I could voice this thought, Juncture called,
"All in favor of declining Gabardine's request?"

"Aye!" nine voices cried.

The room-temperature seemed to rise with my fury. I
undid my uniform's top button.

"Admiral Lechatelierite, we cannot repeat the mistakes
of First Earth," Briggesh responded to my glower. "If Ichthyosis or Nuria were to assist Conflagria with its internal struggles, we'd be no different than the United States
of America, when it intervened in Iraq at the turn of the
twenty-first era—"

"That was an entirely different situation, sir," I cut across
him. He was so stupid, he didn't even know 'century' was
the First Earth word for 'era.' "When the US entered Iraq,
it was introducing a new nation into their war, since Iraq
wasn't responsible for the nine-eleven terrorist attacks.

But, Ichthyosis and Conflagria have already been at war for sixteen ages! We have nothing to lose—"

"Ah, but we do, sir," Briggesh snapped. "The Nurian economy has recessed sharply since the forging of the Second War Pact. We can't afford handouts for Conflagria when we're running ourselves ragged, aiding Ichthyosis. I believe the majority of your fleet is made up of Nurian citizens, Admiral?"

"Ichthyosis is grateful, Mr. President, but I believe a redistribution of funds may be in order. Provide less for us, if you must, to afford concessions for them. Or, simply allow my men to directly aid the Red Revolution—"

The room exploded once again.

"Absolutely not!"

"Outrageous!"

"How dare you!"

"Admiral Lechatelierite," Briggesh bellowed louder than the rest, "if you dare take matters into your own hands, as you've been known to do, and disobey this committee by giving any of your assets to those fire-savages, the GPS on your crafts will alert us, and Nuria will immediately sever ties with Ichthyosis!"

"With all due respect, Mr. President, there's no need for threats," I answered, though sneaking Scarlet a ship full of supplies was exactly what I was thinking of doing as soon as I got home. Inexor could probably hack the GPS…

Juncture banged his gavel. "Order, order! Sirs, a decision has already been made; it's time we move onto our next—"

"We aren't moving on until I hear a substantial justification for this decision!" I growled. I looked expectantly at the Prime Minister. "Sir?"

"If Ichthyosis were fertile enough to provide for another nation, we wouldn't have called to Nuria for help with the war effort to begin with," he said.

"Perhaps we could contract a debt from a neighbor," I said, sweltering in the invisible heat of the conference hall. "Oriya is peaceable, democratic and a friend of Nuria—"

"But, not of Ichthyosis," Briggesh reminded me, acidly. "Ichthyosis's reputation is mud, since its expulsion from the Second Earth Order in eighty-seven. Oriya is the leading power of the Order, and if they got wind of our breach of the Isolationist Laws, Nuria would suffer the same dismal fate. Our nation is risking everything for yours, Admiral. Please, respect that."

My dizziness was progressing to full-on vertigo. I took a long draught of ice-water, but it didn't help.

"Onto the concluding statements," Juncture said. "Nuria shall begin."

"Thank you, Mr. Chairman." Briggesh rose from his seat, clipboard in one hand and cappuccino in the other. "The Democratic-Republic of Nuria has patiently worked with the North Ichthyosis Island for fifteen months. We've armed and outfitted your military; we've filled your store shelves with our goods. While Nuria is proud to serve among such excellence," he yielded me a curt nod, "our patience with Ichthyosis is wearing thin. We believe we've given the Diving Fleet adequate supplies and soldiers to guard our ports from Conflagrian attack. Shall Ichthyosis continue to provide inadequate protection, Nuria will withdraw its manpower from all Ichthyothian bases and halt all wartime production." Briggesh put down his mug. "I would also like to address the current sentiment of the Alliance Committee regarding the rather unorthodox operation of the Nurro-Ichthyothian Diving Fleet." His eyes met mine. "We would like to be completely frank with you, Admiral Lechatelierite: the committee is deeply disappointed in you. We were willing to overlook your past breaches of protocol upon your declaration of victory, five months ago. Now, however, your criminal acts appear unjustifiable."

I stared. "Criminal acts, sir?"

"Yes, Admiral. Your country has decided to press charges for both. You will stand trial for POW abuse and for directly violating executive orders to surrender, last July. Ichthyosis will also be looking into a possible third felony, brought to our attention today. Permitting a Conflagrian mage to serve in the Diving Fleet is illegal and a serious security risk. You don't have the authority to single-handedly make a call like that. The Alliance Committee and the Trilateral Committee should've been consulted beforehand. According to the Second War Pact of the Ninety-Second Age, these crimes warrant your immediate demotion from admiral to commander, and suspension from duty until court-martial, starting the first full business day—"

I sprung to my feet. "Suspend me and the alliance doesn't stand a chance against the System!"

"Sir, you aren't permitted to interrupt the concluding statement of the President!" Juncture shot. "Please be seated."

Briggesh started talking again, but I could no longer hear him over the blood churning in my ears. Faces swam before my eyes. I gasped with an open mouth, but none of the oxygen seemed to reach my lungs. The last thing I remembered was pain shooting through my head before my sight went black.

INEXOR BUIRD

"Heatstroke?" I stared at Cease's small, unconscious form in the hospital bed before me. "He's been to the Conflagrian Fire Pit in the middle of the summer, and you're telling me he got a heatstroke while visiting northern Nuria in the dead of winter?"

Nurse Insouci Raef blinked her cool blue eyes and tucked a stray wisp of platinum-blonde hair behind her ear. "There are other factors at play here, contributing to the deterioration of his overall health."

Deterioration of his overall health? Sure, Cease looked like he dropped a few too many pounds since Scarlet left, but he still showed himself fully capable of kicking some serious Conflagrian tail, so how 'unhealthy' could he possibly be?

"Like what?"

"Well, for starters, there's his low weight, hypertension, PTSD—"

"PTSD?"

"Post-traumatic stress disorder."

"I know what it stands for," I grumbled. "When was that diagnosis made? And, why?" Not that he, like the rest of us, didn't have more than enough reasons to be traumatized. He wouldn't be the first diver to crack. And, PTSD would certainly explain why he spent a good chunk of the autumn puking in the bathroom after battles, like a rookie.

"It isn't a formal diagnosis, only a speculation. Lechatelierite has refused a formal psychiatric evaluation with the medical team, so we're operating on heresy."

"Heresy from who?"

"Colonel Austere. Lechatelierite and Austere have been meeting privately for a couple months, now. What Lechatelierite told the Colonel, the Colonel shared with Dr. Calibre, who concluded Lechatelierite may have PTSD."

I knew Cease had been talking a lot with Austere since October, but I wasn't sure why. It couldn't have been about business, because I was privy to all business matters.

Cease used to share private things with me, too.

"Well, how's he doing, now? What's his prognosis?"

"We brought his body-temperature down to a safe level," she glanced at the monitors all around us. "But, Dr. Calibre isn't sure when he'll wake up." And, with that, she walked away, leaving me with my comatose best friend.

Cease's face, usually so pale, was a blotchy, scarlet red. An odd, black mist seemed to hover around him. I peered at the monitor above his bed and saw his temperature was one-oh-four. Safe level? Barely!

"Sheesh, Cease, what the hell happened at the meeting?" I muttered as I sat at the foot of his bed, feeling guilty for yelling and storming out on him, last night. How stupid were we, to argue over girls we'd never see again, when we had more important things to deal with, like the fact the System was raiding Nurian ports, the alliance was falling apart and our fleet was turning into what the Nurians called a 'circus.' And, Cease was right about me, after all; I'd been distracted since coming home. My performance wasn't up to par. Which added all the more to his stress. His post-traumatic stress.

I looked at the dark circles around his eyes and the way his cheeks seemed to sink up into his face. How much did he weigh, now? A hundred pounds? The puking stopped, but Cease still didn't eat much. At the end of meals, I always saw him turn in near-full trays, if he even showed up to the mess hall in the first place. Most nights, I heard him working on his computer, pounding away at the keyboard, until at least two o'clock.

I breathed out through my nostrils. "Cease," I said, though I knew it was stupid to talk to a person in a coma, "I'm sorry for being off my game, since coming home. I promise I'll work harder from now on; I'll do everything I can to lessen the load you're hauling. And, I'll always stand by you, even if you never think of me as a friend again. Because you'll always be *my* friend, even if you hate my guts and even if the alliance splits and we lose the war." I stood up, hands in my pockets. "And, by the way, Cease," I felt a tingle of nervousness, about to speak words never uttered at Icicle, prohibited under the Laws of Emotional Protection, "happy birthday."

CEASE LECHATELIERITE

Hot sand flew into my face and filled my throat. I coughed into the whipping wind. Wiping my mouth with my floppy, blood-stained sleeve, I squinted at the orange sky, eyes stinging.

What the hell was going on here? Where was I? One minute, I was at the Alliance Conference, and the next, I was in the middle of a…sandstorm…?

I caught sight of a torch soaring through the air, in my direction. With a rush of adrenaline, I dropped to the ground, flames narrowly missing my head. Scrambling to my feet, I scurried to hide behind a nearby mass of hardened lava. Something bounced on my back as I ran. I peered over my shoulder and saw a bow and a quiver of arrows. As I reached for them, my eyes landed on a nasty gash on my forearm, caked with dirt. As the adrenaline ebbed, the wound seared.

So, I was a warrior. A warrior in the middle of a battle unlike I'd ever fought before. Well, no matter the media or terrain, battle was what I did best. Peeking over the boulder, I pulled my bow's taut cord to my chin, released and watched my arrow disappear into the dusty abyss. A scream sounded in the distance as I saw a flash of color—the folds of a robe—falling to the sand.

And, then, a powerful gust quite literally tossed me onto my back. Before I could move, a torch landed mere inches from my face. The wind pushed the flames up my hair and I opened my mouth—

I sat up, yelling, ripping IVs and prongs from my body. I stared down at my arm and saw two, tiny needle-holes where a gaping gash was supposed to be. My white sheets were drenched in cold sweat and my head throbbed. Snow pounded against the frosted window by my bed.

The door opened. "Commander?" a voice croaked, lowly address stinging my ears. "Nice of you to so enthusiastically announce you're awake." It was Nurse Raef.

"Wh-where am I?" I murmured, stupidly. "Shouldn't I be...?" Where exactly *was* I supposed to be?

"You're home, now." She got to work, re-sticking my IVs. "You had a heatstroke in the middle of the Alliance Committee meeting, a couple days ago. Head slammed right into the table. Nasty bruise you came home with."

A couple days? Fear prickled my chest as my mind slowly pieced everything together. I passed out during the conference. Then, I had a dream. No, not a dream. It was too clear and lifelike. It was a vision. It had to be. It was impossible, I knew—the spectral web diffused, and even if it hadn't, I was infrared. But, I was positive this was real. I saw Scarlet. With her magicless hair ablaze.

I swore under my breath, pulse quickening, hands trembling.

"Sir," Raef breathed as my heart-monitor beeped, "please calm down." She moved toward the intercom on the wall. "I'm going get Dr. Calibre."

"No, don't call him; I'm fine!" I snapped. "It's Scarlet who isn't."

She froze, hand poised above the button. "Scarlet? As in, Scarlet July?"

"Do you know any others?" I growled.

"Sir, Icicle hasn't heard a word from or about Scarlet July since she left in August. Even the Reds' appeal to the alliance was written by their co-leader—"

"I saw Scarlet, right now," I cut her off. "She's in battle, and she's hurt. Dead, possibly. Took a torch to the head. I saw it, moments ago. I had a vision."

Raef pulled a clipboard from the foot of my bed and started scribbling on it.

"Commander, please lie back down. Take a deep breath. You just had a hallucination. It's a symptom indicative of post-traumatic stress disorder, which Dr. Calibre has long since suspected you're developing. You still have a fever— you were up to one-oh-six when you had your heatstroke…"

Raef kept talking, but I stopped listening. Heatstroke. Sure, the conference hall felt hot to me, but not hot enough for anyone to develop a fever of one-oh-six.

Of course. That was the body-temperature of a Conflagrian! This couldn't be a coincidence. It was a side-effect of my vision. A momentary result of my connection to Scarlet.

I started yanking prongs and needles from my body.

"Sir! What are you doing?"

What did it look like? "I'm getting the hell out of here."

"Stop that! You're in no condition to leave!"

"I've got business to tend to."

"No, you don't. You've been suspended from service until your court-martial!"

"I know, but I don't give a damn." I jumped to my feet.

She actually took a couple steps back, blue eyes wide. "S-sir, please sit; you could relapse." As if that was what she was really afraid of, here.

"I need to know everything I missed since I went under," I demanded. "Now."

"You're a-asking the wrong person, sir."

"I need to see Inexor, right away."

"Sir, your men are in battle, off the coast of Alcove City."

"Alcove City?"

"The System is stealing from the ports and your fleet is intercepting them, as we speak. That's all I know, sir."

The System was getting more brazen, going so far up the Nurian coast. Previously, all their thefts were contained to the Fervor Gulf. This was a very bad sign.

So, Scarlet was burning alive and Inexor was leading our circus of a fleet in the Briny Ocean, at this very moment. And, I was stuck here, in the hospital. Suspended from duty. What would become of the Nurro-Ichthyothian Resistance without me? What would become of the Red Revolution without Scarlet? My hands were completely tied. I couldn't do anything to help anyone. I couldn't stand this powerlessness, this complete lack of control.

Without warning, the floor slanted beneath my feet. I moaned, eyes rolling to the back of my head...

I heard voices behind me, gathering intensity. The language was familiar but oddly incomprehensible. Something hard and sharp jabbed me in the back. I opened my eyes and beheld the interior of a tiny sub. I looked down at my dark-orange flight-suit and olive-green gloves. *Now* what was going on?

I slowly thought things through. I was at sea. The pressure on my back was a gun. Enemy soldiers had infiltrated my ship. I glanced down at my belt and saw my holster was empty.

Suddenly, my hands felt like they were on fire. I called out as I pulled off my gloves. Flashes of yellow and green light emitted from my palms. What was happening to me? And, how could I make it stop?

Before I could call out, the burning ebbed, replaced by strength. Strength as I'd never felt before. I curled and uncurled my fingers. These hands were powerful enough to snap necks. I could do it. I should.

But, something inside me rebelled. *Its one thing to shoot down their ships,* said a terrified voice in my head, *but quite another to break their necks with your hands.*

No, there was no difference, I argued back. I did it before and it wasn't a big deal. Without a gun, what choice did I have? This was war, after all. Either kill or be killed.

I whipped around and knocked my enemies to the floor with a couple, swift punches. Two white suits lay limp at my feet. They wore silver helmets with the visors up. Wait a minute—

They were Nurro-Ichthyothian divers! But, it was too late to stop myself; in horror, I watched as my glowing hands simultaneously grabbed their throats and broke their necks.

I looked into their eyes. They were my own soldiers. Nurian. I just killed two of my own men. Ecivon Wen and Tnerruc Ruetama, from Nurtic Leavesleft's unit.

I pulled off my helmet and gulped the stale, hot air. Wen's dead body twitched and his visor slid shut. And, I saw my own reflection in his shiny, tinted glass.

A stranger's face stared back at me. He had amber-gold eyes, tan skin, a square jaw and dark copper hair that stuck up in all directions.

AMBREK COPPERTUS

System Water Forces Captain Anapes Patrici finally decided I was ready. He finally recognized the value of my astounding eye-hand-coordination coupled with my inside knowledge of the Nordic military—knowledge acquired from none other than the former Second-in-Command of the Ichthyothian Diving Fleet herself. So, this morning, a handful of his men broke into Red Headquarters and 'kidnapped' me so I could participate in today's raid of the Alcove City ports. My very first real sea battle.

Over the past five months, Scarlet had told me many tales of her days in the Diving Fleet. She said, while the Ichthyothians weren't exactly known for their creativity or resourcefulness, they were incredibly sharp and organized, operating with impeccable precision and dangerous accuracy. In addition to their remarkable skill and strategy, they were well-outfitted. No longer spectrally reinforced to allow for deep-sea diving, the System's cloth flightsuits were just good for sitting inside cockpits, while the Ichthyothian 'arrhythmic' suits protected perfectly against water pressure. Scarlet also told me the Ichthyothian government abducted male children *at birth* and raised them in military academies until they either flunked out and became normal civilian kids or graduated around sixteen and were thrown into combat. Lechatelierite himself graduated at ten and was made commander of the elite Diving Fleet by fifteen. For Tincture's sake, August was the first time I ever wore a System Water Forces uniform, and I was about to face the best fighters Second Earth had to offer, led by a man who was literally a living legend.

So, yes, I was nervous as hell.

Piloting a stolen Nordic sub, I now made my way through the cobalt blue depths of the Briny Ocean, heading north, alongside nineteen other subs and one carrier. I tailed Anapes closely. Before the Crystal was destroyed, his aura was purple and his source was his internal organs. Pre-diffusion, he was immune to disease and infection but, post-diffusion, he got sick at least once a month. I guessed, with spectrum doing all the heavy lifting, his actual immune system never needed to develop.

His voice sounded on my intercom, "Coppertus, my 'radar' is picking up sixteen of those long, thin shuttles and one of those big, flying ships that looks like a manta ray. They're seven miles to our north."

I exhaled through gritted teeth. Crimson would roll over in her grave if she knew how stupid her replacement was. "Sir, the 'long, thin shuttles' are called crystallines and the 'manta ray' is called 'vitreous silica.' Crystallines are swifter and more maneuverable but have less firepower. If the vitreous silica has blue stripes on its wings, it's one of the older, air- or sea-only models. The newer models are convertible. You should be aware of the basics, Captain."

"I am," he retorted acidly, "but, thanks for the little lesson. And, may I remind you, *I* don't spend the majority of my time in the presence of an Ichthyothian tool!"

"You really don't need to yell into the intercom," I said, calmly. "The Nordics built in an automatic volume adjuster to regulate the intensity level of all transmitted sound."

"Quit lecturing me," he shot.

I rolled my eyes. "Sorry, sir."

"We outnumber them," he noted a moment later, voice dripping with satisfaction.

Idiot. "Sir, do you know how many men a vitreous silica can carry? And, it's far more difficult to hit an individual diver dropping through the sky or swimming in the sea than it is to hit a ship—"

"I *have* fought Ichthyothians before, you know," Anapes cut across me, tone chilly. "And, unlike you, I've actually *seen* men dive from a carrier, so you don't need to warn me. I was simply making an observation that they have seventeen crafts, counting the manta ray, while we have twenty-one."

Couldn't he see those numbers didn't matter? We were going up against a diving fleet, and we *couldn't dive!* Not to mention, several of our top soldiers absconded to the Reds when the spectrum diffused, which was why there was room in the frontlines for rookies like me. And, worst of all, we didn't have our *real* leader here today. My sister. The odds were stacked against us.

I was so anxious, my hands actually shook on the joy-stick. I doubted I'd ever get used to how frail and unsteady diffused hands were. I was accustomed to perfect dexterity. Until July thirty-first, I never even knew what it was like to drop something on accident. But, now, it seemed like whatever I touched slid between my fingers like sand. My hands felt so sluggish and clumsy. Could I face a fleet of technology-wielding, ice-faring, military geniuses while I was inexperienced and without a photon of spectrum?

Yes. For Crimson.

By now, the Ichthyothian Fleet was visible to the naked eye. I saw sixteen crystallines darting about; they seemed impossible to follow with my gaze, let alone my crosshairs. Here and there, I caught flashes of white—the 'surface-riders' streamlining between shuttles. Other divers stayed above water, tossing one another into the air and firing at our carrier. I took a deep breath and dove into the scene, my hunger for vengeance against Lechatelierite dampened a little by nerves.

The battle wore on. Upon arrival, the Ichthyothian Fleet did indeed look impressive to my virgin eyes. Halfway through the second hour, however, I realized I wasn't having as much of a hard time staying alive and wreaking havoc as I thought I would. Turned out, the enemy's performance was sloppier than Scarlet led me to expect. When divers deployed from the vitreous silica, several dropped their weapons in mid-fall and crashed into the water like flailing children. The crystalline pilots seemed to be following their example; they traveled in wobbling paths, sometimes missing entire groups of hurtling surface-riders. Most shocking of all, the fleet lacked a cohesive strategy—it seemed like everyone was doing pretty much whatever they wanted—which signified poor leadership on Lechatelierite's part.

This was the best Ichthyosis had to offer? Scarlet led me to believe Lechatelierite was some sort of god of warfare. For Tincture's sake, I was supposed to be the green one, here.

"Is it just me, or is this too easy?" I asked Anapes.

"It's not just you," he grunted. "But, I'm not complaining."

"There must be a reason for it, sir. If this isn't normal, something's up."

A crystalline darted very closely to my left, nearly whacking my wing.

"Watch it, Coppertus!" Anapes snapped. "Don't get cocky."

I descended sharply. The crystalline, unshaken, circled back and almost grated me again. If the Diving Fleet was off its game today, this pilot was an exception. The shuttle whipped about in dizzying loops, nothing but a little dash of grey in my sights. How on earth would I get a target-lock? Every time he doubled back, he came closer to scraping me. And, then, I heard a series of *thuds.*

"Coppertus, you have four men on your dorsal fin!" Anapes yelled.

"Can you shoot them off?"

"Not without shooting you down. Drop to the reef, spin and chafe them off."

"That won't bust my ship?"

"You bet it will, but not as much as if I were to open fire."

I didn't think I truly understood the meaning of the word 'dilemma,' until now. I dove, listening to the sounds of the surface-riders crawling across my hull. A second before I would've crashed, I flattened my joystick to the right. As I barrel-rolled, my fins scraped into the coral.

'CRITICAL DAMAGE WARNING' flashed on my panel.

"Sir, my shields are at seven percent," I called to Anapes from miles beneath the raging battle.

"Head home, Coppertus. The rest of us will be following suit soon—we've just about finished wrangling a decent loot from the ports, wiping the floor with the Ichthyothians while we were at it."

"Glad to hear it, sir. Coppertus out."

"Alright, men," he called universally, "I think we can call this a victory. Back to base!"

THUD.

What was that? My pulse skyrocketed. Was someone still on me? How did anyone survive my maneuver?

I heard the bang of double-doors breaking open and the thumps of two men dropping through. Before I could even turn in my seat, I felt a muzzle poke my back. My body tensed; I could feel goosebumps rise on my arms, beneath my suit.

"Yield your vessel or we'll fire!"

What language was that? It sounded like a distorted form of Ichthyothian—the vowel sounds were strangely warped. Why would this diver speak to me in any tongue but his own?

I wasn't stupid enough to try to fight two armed divers while diffused and unarmed. Since the System stole all its tech from the Nordics, not everybody in the Water Forces had a sidearm. I was too green to be issued such a precious resource. I froze, bracing myself for an iron slug through my back. Crimson would be so ashamed; I was going to die during my very first sea battle!

"Yield now, Conflagrian, or we'll fire!" the same voice repeated.

I only understood one word: 'Conflagrian.' Why weren't they killing me?

"Stand aside, prisoner," the other chimed in.

My heart leapt as I recognized another word: 'prisoner' was the same in Ichthyothian as it was in whatever language they were speaking. They wanted to capture rather than kill me straight off? So, I had a chance!

"I don't think he understands us, Ecivon," the man to my right blurted incomprehensibly to his comrade. "Do you know any Conflagrian?"

"Are you kidding?"

"Well, try Ichthyothian, then!"

"I don't really know much Ichthyothian, Tnerruc!"

"Well, neither do I!"

They sounded like they were arguing. Seriously? What a time to be arguing!

My hands suddenly went rigid, searing from wrist to fingertip. I fought the urge to scream as I pulled off my gloves, amber and copper light filling my sight. I recognized what was happening. But, no, it was impossible…

I balled my powerful, glowing fists. I was finally myself again. A hand mage.

Snap their necks, said a voice in my head.

Instantly, terror struck me. I couldn't believe I'd even think such a thought. There was no way I'd do it. Because it was one thing to shoot down their ships, but quite another to break their necks with your hands.

No, there's no difference, the voice argued back. *Without a gun, what choice do you have? This is war, after all. Either kill or be killed.*

I jumped from my seat and whipped around to face the men. Visors up, they looked at me with wide, scared eyes. I balled my fists and knocked them to the floor. Then, I watched in horror as my fingers curled around their throats and snapped their necks. Right through their arrhythmic suits.

I threw off my helmet, gasping with an open mouth, corpses at my feet. I just killed with my bare hands. Literally, with my bare hands. I was defending myself in combat; I knew I did the right thing. I did what I had to. But, the thought still made me sick.

SCARLET JULY

A torch landed in the sand, right beside my head. Instantly, the wind carried the flames up my sprawled hair. A scream tore from my throat as images spun before my eyes. The flutter of blue wings. The purple glow of a throat. The ripple of black hair in the moonlight. The sunshine of a yellow wrist. The pearly shimmer of white locks. The copper shine of a hand. A handsome smile on an angular face, framed by dark, tousled hair…

With a brilliant flash of red light, the pain vanished. The fire on my head was now nothing more than warm breath. I could see between each individual fleck of sand billowing in the storm. And, my hair was alive, moving like fingers, feeling the wind filter between strands.

I jumped up from behind the boulder and ran across the field, eyes shooting fireballs. Arrows flew my way but my hair snagged them and chucked them right back. I dropped into the enemy trench, screaming as my fiery locks sliced through flesh. When they were all dead, I climbed out and threw myself back across no-man's land, to where Fair and the others awaited, staring with open mouths.

And then, without warning, my body felt as though plunged into the North Septentrion Sea, naked. Red mist seeped from my eyes and hair. I tumbled into the hot sand. As quickly as my aura crystallized, it diffused.

INSOUCI RAEF

Lechatelierite hit the floor. He lay on his side, silver eyes wide, arms and legs thrashing. Heatstroke, hypertension, hallucinations and now a seizure, too?

Suddenly, his body went limp and his eyes snapped shut. I approached him, nervously, and scooped him up. He was easy to lift. Too easy. It was like the war literally ate away at him until there was next to nothing left. I placed him on his bed and checked his vital signs. This man had no business scuba diving and sailing the seas and killing mages. He needed rest, peace and longterm medical care.

I was about to reattach his second IV when he must've had a muscle spasm; his right hand sprung up and clocked my jaw. I cried out. Eyes still shut, he grabbed my neck. No, these weren't spasms; he was trying to kill me! Gasping, I stabbed his arm with the needle, forcing him to release me. I backed away, hyperventilating, feeling the aftereffect of his fingers on my throat. I jumped when he sat up quick as gunfire, banging his head on a low-hanging light fixture. His face was paler than the walls and sweat beads stood out on his forehead like crystals. Maybe fear was making me crazy, but I swore I could see a strange, black mist hover around him. He balled his fists, doubled over and panted. Then, he turned his dangerous glare on me.

Fighting the urge to wet my pants and run away screaming, I drew my pistol and aimed it at his head.

"Don't move!" I cried. "I won't let you have another attempt at my life!"

His eyebrows scrunched. "What?"

Hands shaking, I aimed at his leg instead. If he tried to hurt me again, I didn't want to kill him, only stop him. I wasn't about to kill the Leader of the Nurro-Ichthyothian Resistance.

"Hands up!"

He didn't obey. He just stared off into the distance, face pensive. He seemed wholly unfazed by being at my gunpoint. Of course, how silly I must've looked to him, compared to the horrors he faced at sea.

"That's it!" He looked down at his hands. "That wasn't an attempt at your life, I responding to my vision!"

What? "Hallucination!" I screeched.

He stood and headed for the door. As I stepped in his way, I actually had to concentrate on my bladder so I wouldn't let go.

"Sit down!"

"Ma'am, if my men aren't back from battle yet, I need to speak with Colonel Austere, now."

"You won't leave this room!"

He looked at my pistol with an annoyed air. "Will you put that thing away? I'm not going to hurt you, now that I'm conscious, and it's a bit distracting—"

The door behind me opened.

"Hey, Cease, you're awake!" In came Inexor Buird in a wet diving suit, tracking saltwater all over the polished, hospital floor. His brows shot to his buzzed hairline. "What's going on in here?"

"Inexor!" Lechatelierite cried. "You won't believe what I just saw. We need to talk."

Was the Commander actually making conversation with a third party while at gunpoint?

Buird blinked. "Um, Cease, why is Mrs. Raef aiming a pistol at you? And, why's your arm bleeding?"

"Never mind that; round up the unit leaders!"

I holstered my weapon; there really was no point. Plus, I was safe, now—Buird could always intervene if things got violent. He had, what, a hundred pounds on Lechatelierite?

"What did you just see?" Buird looked around the room, nonplussed. "You mean, like, in here?"

"No. Yes." Lechatelierite's chest rose and fell as he rubbed his temples. "It's complicated. I'd prefer to explain it to everyone at once."

"Do you have a bad prognosis or something? Are you okay?" Buird pressed.

"No, he isn't," I piped. "He just had a seizure and—"

"I'm fine!" Lechatelierite snapped. "Inexor, let's go. You can fill me in on how the battle went, on the way."

"Sir, you've been suspended from duty," I reminded Lechatelierite.

"W-what?" Buird sputtered. "If Cease is suspended from duty—that means I–I—"

"That means you're going to stop standing there, blub-bering like a Childhood Program trainee, and act like a damn leader for a change. Move!" Lechatelierite barked.

Buird nodded and scurried away. A prickle of fear shot through me as I was left alone with Lechatelierite again.

He looked at me with those disorienting, steel eyes. "I'm meeting with my men," he grunted. "Try and stop me." And, with that, he pushed past me and bolted right out the door.

FAIR GABARDINE

Scarlet's head was on fire! She writhed in the sand, cries of anguish piercing the dusty wind. This was it. My best friend was burning to death, before my eyes. As if on cue, she fell still and silent. My breath caught in my throat.

And then, like magic, she stood up, flames still leaping from her scalp. I stared, wondering if I was going mad. Scarlet ran out from behind the lava boulder and scurried across no-man's land, shooting fireballs from her eyes. She jumped into the enemy trench.

My own hair began to tremble. White light filled my sight as heat surged to my scalp—

TRAITOR! TOOL of the ICHTHYOTHIANS! THIEF of our spectrum!

I leapt to my feet. I was going to kill Scarlet July.

But, before I could take a step, ice assaulted my head as white mist leached from my hair. In the distance, I saw Scarlet leap from the trench, screaming. Halfway across the field, she fell to the ground, stirring a cloud of sand. When the dust settled, her aura was gone.

I ran to her. "Scarlet," I breathed, pulling her back up.

"Was that…did you…spectrum?" she panted.

"Yes!" In a matter of seconds, my aura crystallized then diffused. And, with it, came a terrifying wave of loyalty to the System. I swallowed.

"No, no, no." Scarlet grasped her hair with trembling hands. "The Crystal is destroyed! It's impossible for the spectral web to exist without it!" She grabbed the front of my robe and shouted right into my face, "The Crystal's destroyed—I DESTROYED IT! The web's DIFFUSED!" And, she threw herself into my arms, weeping loudly.

"Scarlet, please." I stroked her hair, still warm from the magic that touched it for an instant. "That burst of spectrum saved your life!"

"What's my life compared to the revolution? If the magic crystallizes for good, it's all over. That'd be it, for Conflagria!"

Enemy trench empty and all immediate threat averted, our fellow Red warriors began to step out into no-man's land and cluster around us. They stared at Scarlet in confusion and awe.

"How?" Prunus Persica breathed. Once upon a time, he was a skin mage with a peach aura. Though, diffusion left him no less handsome than before. "How did it happen? And, how come only you two were affected?"

"You didn't feel anything?" I gaped.

Murmurs and head-shakes surrounded us. "None of us did," he said.

I looked at Scarlet.

"No one in the trench could fight me back," she croaked.

Nothing made sense. Nothing at all. We stood in silent shock, wind and sand beating our backs.

AMBREK COPPERTUS

Shuddering all over, I nearly crash-landed in the hangar. I scrambled out of the cockpit and toppled onto the platform, throwing off my helmet. Amber and copper light erupted from my open palms as my whole body felt as though pierced with a thousand icicles.

That pain was familiar. That's exactly how it felt when Scarlet and Lechatelierite destroyed the Core Crystal on that fateful July day, five months ago.

Everyone stared. "Spectrum!" someone yelled, unnecessarily.

"It…it's…diffusing!" I cried.

My comrades watched as I writhed on the deck, iridescent mist pouring from my every pore. At last, the final photons flickered and extinguished. I wrung my hands.

"Coppertus?" I heard Anapes's voice. "Coppertus, what happened?"

"Sir, my aura just…crystallized all of a sudden, at sea," I panted, too weak to even sit up. It felt rude and awkward to address my captain lying down, but I couldn't move.

Anapes dropped to his knees beside me, eyes wide. Wait, why wasn't he throwing up purple light?

"Was anyone else affected?" I choked.

Silence.

"No one?"

"No, Coppertus," Anapes said. "Just you."

* * *

I returned to Red Headquarters late that night, a triumphant POW escapee.

"Ambrek!" Scarlet screeched, throwing herself at me the moment she opened the door. I wrapped my arms around her slender waist, cursing myself silently for enjoying her touch so much. "Where did they take you? How did you escape? Tell us everything!"

I followed her inside, dragging my feet. There was no need to feign exhaustion—I really did feel like I was on the brink of passing out. Scarlet brought me a glass of dragon milk and a bowl of taro root while Fair fetched me a torch.

"I was held captive on a System sub. They went to battle in the Briny Ocean."

"A *sea* battle? So, you saw the Ichthyothians!" Scarlet bounded toward me, sloshing milk onto her robe. "How's Cease's fleet doing?" Her eyes seemed to light up at the sound of her ex-commander's name. It was all I could do to keep the anger from my face. Even Fair looked a little irritated.

"Um, well, it's not like I could see much, from where I was held," I said slowly, taking a sip of milk and sitting down on my tarp. "But, I do know the Ichthyothians lost. Got away with maybe half their crystallines."

"Maybe half?" Scarlet echoed, red lashes quivering. "They did that badly? How?" She sank to the floor, at my feet. "Cease never loses."

I bit into a taro. "Sorry, Scarlet, but I wasn't impressed with your old fleet. They were sloppy. I know Cease is supposed to be a big deal and all, but honestly, I don't get what the hype is about."

"Hey, don't get angry at him!" Scarlet folded her arms across her chest. If she still had her eye magic, I'd be ashes on the floor, right about now. "You can't pin this all on Cease. The majority of his fleet are Nurian rookies, after all."

"Nurian?" Wait a minute, was *that* why the surface-riders who infiltrated my ship didn't speak Ichthyothian? "How could there be Nurians in the Ichthyothian Military?"

Scarlet blinked. "I thought I told you before; Ichthyosis and Nuria are allies."

My stomach disappeared. "What? When did that happen?"

"Over an age ago. Cease is the one who wrote the treaty."

Of course, he was. "But…what about the Isolationist Laws? Is Nuria blacklisted now, or what?"

"No. The Order doesn't know."

And, neither did the System, apparently. I couldn't believe it. This changed everything. "Why would Nuria do such a thing?"

"Come on, Ambrek, look at a map. Nuria is *sandwiched* between two nations who've been at each other's throats for sixteen ages. Before the alliance was forged, Ichthyosis was on the brink of defeat. And, with Ichthyosis out of the way, guess who the System's likely to target next?"

This explained so much! Like why the Diving Fleet was so enormous, now. They had Nuria's manpower.

Scarlet cocked a crimson brow at me. "How else did you think I could enlist when I lived in Alcove City?"

"I don't know." I dipped a chunk of taro in my milk—a sight that always made Fair shudder. "I figured you moved to Ichthyosis after hearing about the war from the Nurian media, or something. You know, television and computers and stuff—I imagine word gets around a lot faster on 'technological' nations."

"Under the Isolationist Laws, the Nurian media wouldn't cover the Ichthyo-Conflagrian war at all, unless Nuria were already directly involved," she said slowly and incredulously, as though I were the world's greatest idiot.

I could care less if Scarlet thought I was stupid as a sca-brous. All I could think about now was how soon I could get this intel to the Mage Castle.

"How did you escape?" Fair brought the conversation back on track. Damn her.

I swallowed. "You won't believe this, but I was able to fight…with magic."

"So, it happened to you, too," Scarlet breathed.

Too?

"Scarlet and I, we both felt a surge," Fair said. "Just the two of us. Just for a moment."

"Mine lasted a few hours," I blurted.

They stared.

"You said you were in the Briny Ocean?" Scarlet pressed, green eyes urgent.

"Sort of. Where the Briny Ocean meets the Fervor Sea. It was warm water."

"Nearer to the surface or the seafloor?"

What an odd question. "Seafloor."

"*That's it!*" she screeched. "You were physically close to it, and Fair and I were also impacted because we're spec-trally twined to you."

"What are you talking about?" Fair asked.

"Close to what?" I demanded.

"Last August, on our way home from Icicle, I threw s-something overboard." She gulped. "I thought, after the diffusion, it was nothing but a powerless fragment, but—"

I rounded on her. "Wait, you had a piece of the Core Crystal?" And, she tossed it into the ocean!?

"A System guard gave it to me the day I was deported. I held onto it for six ages without knowing what it was."

"Hold the torch," Fair said. "You're saying an *active* fragment of the *Core Crystal* is at the bottom of the Briny Ocean, *right now?*"

"Yes!"

"The System is out there all the time!" Fair yelled. "Sooner or later, if they haven't already, they're going to notice, just like Ambrek, that passing a particular spot makes their auras miraculously crystallize. And, if they figure out why and find the shard, all they'd have to do to restore the spectral web is drop it in the Fire Pit. It'll take root and grow!"

And, the only person on Second Earth who'd be powerful enough to destroy the Crystal—again—was Scarlet, the Multi-Source Enchant. So, if the Crystal got restored and Scarlet got killed, that'd be it. The spectral web—and the System's dominion—would be back for good. There'd be nothing anyone could do about it. It'd be victory, complete victory.

I couldn't tell the System about the shard. Not yet. If I did, whoever they assigned to help me find it would share—or perhaps take all—the credit. I wanted to seize it and throw it into the Pit myself, becoming the most important figure in Conflagrian history. I'd be the man who single-handedly rescued the System and restored the auras of all magekind. I'd be the savior of my people.

Searching for a tiny fragment on the seafloor would be like trying to find a pebble in a pile of dragon dung. It was impossible. To me. But, it wouldn't be, for Scarlet. Because, once in reasonable range of the shard's emission, she would have her eye magic.

And, once I was done using her to get the crystal, I'd kill her.

CEASE LECHATELIERITE

My officers regarded me with critical eyes as I stood before them in the lecture hall and relayed what I saw in my visions.

Illia Frappe, the Ichthyothian leader of unit three, gave me a wary look, folding his arms across his chest. "Sir, there's no spectral web, anymore. And, even if there were, you're not a mage. You can't have visions. If Scarlet July were the one saying this, maybe then I'd believe it."

"Even before we met, Scarlet had a vision of me," I said. "Of the battle in which the System introduced the Underwater Fire." At this, everyone seemed to sit up a little straighter. I never spoke about that battle—the black mark on my record. "Not only could she see through my eyes, she could insert thoughts into my mind. So, yes, it *is* somehow possible for 'infrareds' to access the spectral web."

What I really couldn't understand was why I'd have a vision of a random System pilot I didn't know. Maybe we'd meet soon? I figured Scarlet could break the rules and twine to me before our first actual encounter because she was the Multi-Source Enchant and had dominion over the spectral web. The natural laws of spectroscopy didn't always apply to her. But, they should to this hand mage. Unless…he knew Scarlet and our connection was through her? That seemed a bit far-fetched. Why would Scarlet twine to an enemy soldier, anyway?

"Sir, if the Core Crystal was destroyed in July," Illia said, "how could this pilot have an aura? Where's it coming from?"

"Maybe the System made a new magic-generator, or something," suggested Dither Maine, the Nurian sub-leader of unit ten.

"Or, maybe, a new crystal is naturally cultivating in the Fire Pit," proposed Quiesce Tacit, the Ichthyothian leader of unit four.

Illia snapped his fingers. "Yes, and the spectral emissions are inconsistent because the new crystal is still young and small."

Nurtic Leavesleft, the Nurian leader of unit two, looked at me, hazel eyes thoughtful. "Sir, you said the pilot felt really surprised when his aura crystallized. Don't a lot of people use the Fire Pit on a daily basis? If there was a new crystal growing in there, wouldn't everyone know already? Wouldn't they expect these intermittent bursts of spectrum?"

Ecivon Wen and Tnerruc Ruetama, the two surface-riders I—or, rather, the hand mage pilot—killed were friends of Leavesleft's from Alcove City. According to their files, the three were neighbors and classmates. Wen and Ruetama arrived at Icicle three months after Leavesleft. Leavesleft was also very close to Scarlet. He always hovered around her, and he sought to protect her from the likes of Amok Kempt. I even wondered for a while if Scarlet would choose to love him over me. Leavesleft had a very readable face for a soldier, and when I described my visions at the start of the meeting, his cheeks reddened and he looked like he wanted to vomit. He just lost three people he cared about.

"Not necessarily, Leavesleft," answered Arrhyth Link, the Nurian sub-leader of unit eleven. "If you recall, it's not easily visible through the flames. Only Scarlet could see it, with her eye magic."

Link never missed an opportunity to talk about the infiltration, as if his mere day in Conflagrian airspace gave him sage wisdom and expertise he needed to constantly bestow upon us all. Never mind that Leavesleft was there too, playing a much more active role in the mission than him. All Link did was ride around in the vitreous silica, looking over a couple unconscious bodies—Scarlet passed out right after destroying the Crystal and I passed out right after bringing her aboard.

"I'm not talking about noticing it by sight." Leavesleft shook his head. "What I mean is, if there's another crystal in the Pit, wouldn't everyone feel random blips of spectrum all the time, especially when closer to the Pit? The pilot was really shocked when his magic came back. So, Conflagrians don't expect their auras to suddenly crystallize, every now and then. And, I don't think the new powersource is in the Fire Pit, either—why'd the pilot feel such a strong surge over a thousand miles from Ardor Village? Maybe there's something in the Briny Ocean causing it. Something the people of Conflagria don't know about."

Leavesleft sounded like he was onto something. And, he seemed like the only one here putting in real effort into figuring things out. He took my visions seriously, while everyone else seemed tired, irritated and convinced I was wasting their time with stupid delusions. Of all my officers, he alone trusted me.

"How could a spectral crystal form anywhere but the Fire Pit?" Illia asked, giving Leavesleft an annoyed look.

"The Pit would clearly be the only environment on Second Earth conducive to its evolution," Quiesce agreed.

Leavesleft held his pencil as though it were a joystick. "Well, you're assuming the original Crystal evolved, in the first place."

Oh boy.

"Irrelevant," I snapped. I refused to let the discussion break out into a creation-versus-evolution argument. We needed to stay on topic.

"It's not irrelevant," Link insisted, siding with Leavesleft, of course. As usual, the group was splitting into Nurians versus Ichthyothians. "Evolution's supposed to take billions of ages—how'd a new crystal evolve in five months? And, from what?"

"We're not talking about anything as complex as the biological evolution of one species into another through natural selection," Quiesce responded, icily. "Just the formation of a small crystal."

"A crystal that's probably as elaborate as any life form," Leavesleft said. "It generates an intricate spectral network that sustains the magnetic fields of every mage to have ever lived."

"Yeah, if anything so complex were to evolve, it'd take far longer than five months!" Link said. "And, it wouldn't just spontaneously generate, out of nowhere!"

Inexor leaned forward. "Well, did you consider that magic could possibly alter or accelerate the process?"

"And, where do you think this 'magic' comes from, in the first place?" Maine shot.

"SILENCE!" I erupted.

The room went dead quiet.

"Not another word on this stupid tangent!" One by one, I glowered at Leavesleft, Link, Maine, Illia, Inexor and Quiesce. "Understood?"

Flustered, Illia folded his arms and glared at Leavesleft, who dropped his gaze to his palms and sighed. Quiesce set his surly eyes on Link, who turned to Maine and shrugged. Inexor just leaned back and rolled his eyes. The room was tense—all the creativity that'd been flowing freely was now abruptly stifled by the lingering air of disagreement.

"Maybe there isn't another crystal, at all," Link piped, lamely. He was answered with a dozen cold, Ichthyothian stares.

I decided to temporarily bring the discussion away from the mystery of the spectral web's recrystallization. It was time for yet another unpleasant subject: the most recent battle. I wasn't sure why we lost. I needed each officer to explain the logistics of his unit's performance. I began with Inexor, who piloted the vitreous silica. I asked him to give me an overview of the battle—why it got going in the first place and what his strategy was.

He took a long draught of ice water before getting up. He shifted on his feet, looking, for all the world, like a six-age-old cold-called in Colonel Austere's class. As he spoke, the Ichthyothians sat still as stones, eyes vacant. But, their internal irritation was evident in the way their temples pulsed and their knuckles went white as they gripped their mechanical pencils. The Nurians looked more anxious than frustrated and they weren't good at hiding it. They shuffled a lot in their seats and looked around at the floor, the ceiling, the door, the table, the person across from them—just about anywhere but at me or Inexor. It didn't take a military genius to figure why the Nurians were behaving like nervous, Childhood Program trainees about to take their first solo flights.

They felt guilty. They felt responsible for the loss. They wished Inexor would just shut up already and stop trying to make things sound better than they really were.

"So, basically, what you're trying to say is, you had no plan," I interrupted Inexor's babble. "You basically let the unit leaders do whatever they wanted."

Inexor was silent.

I clenched my jaw. "Sit down," I ordered.

He sat.

I activated the large screen behind me and quickly sketched up a hypothetical plan of attack. I pointed to where two crystallines orbited below an airborne vitreous silica.

"Maine, explain why I have these two shuttles in a circuit, near to the surface."

"To surround the enemy fighters?"

"Incorrect. Buird?"

"To fire in all directions?"

"Incorrect. Frappe?"

"To provide the surface-riders with a safe 'launching pad' for the spin-toss maneuver?"

"Incorrect. Tacit?"

"To provide a streamlining 'zone' for the surface-riders?"

"Closer, but still no. Leavesleft?"

"To serve as a protective barrier for the soldiers who dove from the vitreous silica and are just entering the water," he answered, firmly.

"Correct. Dozens of divers from the vitreous silica were lost in this battle alone. And, most of them were killed by enemy fire, the instant they entered the water. During the drop itself, they're difficult to see or hit, and they can do a lot of damage as they spin and shoot. Once underwater, they can surface-ride. But, the *moment* they break the surface is the moment they're most vulnerable, as that's when they must stop tumbling and shooting, positioning themselves in an easily-visible, vertical arrow. A crystalline can take a lot more heat than a diving suit, so at least two shuttles should surface and form protective circuits around the main landing-terrain of the divers, to intercept enemy fire." I snapped off the screen. "I shouldn't have to explain these kinds of basics to you." I folded my arms. "Unit two, report."

Leavesleft rose to his feet.

"You were piloting crystalline two, correct?"

"Yes, sir."

He went on to describe his unit's strategy, including how he'd intended for his men to infiltrate an enemy fighter and take a System pilot captive. Pre-diffusion, we typically targeted enemy surface-riders for capture, not pilots. It was much easier to snag a lone swimmer in the sea than it was to hijack a ship. But, the Water Forces could no longer deep-sea dive, as their magicless flightsuits weren't equipped to withstand water-pressure. I knew, however, it was only a matter of time before the System would dissect the few Nordic diving suits they stole and learn to duplicate our pressure-resistant 'arrhythmic' fabric.

Leavesleft's plot was thwarted, of course. Because I gave the enemy pilot the idea to use his inexplicable burst of spectrum to snap his attackers' necks. I was surprised by how much the pilot resisted my idea and how anxious it made him. He was outnumbered, at gunpoint and in immediate, life-threatening danger, yet he didn't want to use the only weapon he had—his magical hands—to defend himself because that would be too gross and scary. Seriously. He would've died if I weren't there to save his ass. The man was supposed to be a soldier, for crying out loud. What kind of soldier would put his own life—and his nation's security, if captured—in jeopardy because fighting back would be disgusting and frightening? This kid was obviously an amateur of amateurs, if the possibility of getting his hands dirty shook him up so much. This was war. What did he expect war to look like? Sterile and clean?

"Thank you, Leavesleft," I said, once he was finished. "Unit three, report."

Illia rose to his feet, brown eyes hard. Things between us got a bit strained since I unexpectedly returned from my brief captivity last July and walked in on him mouthing off to Scarlet in front of the entire fleet, calling my decision to kamikaze into the Fervor Base futile and cowardly. I didn't demote him because he was a brilliant tactician and a skilled fighter—attributes that seemed to be in short supply, these days—but, my respect for him never fully recovered.

"My unit's primary objective was to use the spin-toss maneuver to take out the enemy carrier. While we didn't manage to destroy it, we did inflict severe damage."

After some prodding on my part, he finally admitted he saw a lot of sloppy throws, rendering flyers disoriented far too long after execution. The result? Over half the surface-riders in his unit got killed. And, all of them were Nurian.

"Officers, after we're finished here, round up your units at the pool for a review of the spin-toss. We've gone over it a number of times already, but apparently, a team of pre-teen, cheerleader girls can throw better than my men." I wasn't sure all the base-raised divers would understand the reference; I'd heard about cheerleaders from Link, a little while back. Apparently, he had a romantic relationship with one in high school.

Illia sank to his seat.

"Unit four, report!"

Quiesce stood, boredom in his pale blue eyes. Quiesce had an analytical mind, a reserved nature and a particularly low tolerance for stupidity and for Nurians. He rarely bantered during off-hours, speaking only when business mandated. Friendships at Icicle were illegal under the Laws of the Emotional Protection, but every man here, Nurian and Ichthyothian alike, still tended to gravitate to at least one other person, however subtly. Except Quiesce. He kept to himself.

In this battle, his unit was one of several to deploy from the vitreous silica. In few words, he described the nightmare that unfolded. Inexor's unsteady piloting threw several of his men out of the shaft before they were ready. While most of the Ichthyothians managed to recover their dives, none of the Nurians did. They fell like sleet, dropping their weapons and crash-landing on their shoulders, backs, bellies or sides. And, since no crystalline pilot thought to orbit, they were completely exposed. Every single Nurian in his unit was killed.

The afternoon passed like a session of slow torture. I listened to the reports of my officers and saw there was no coordination whatsoever between units. It was as if several small armies launched into the sea rather than one fleet with multiple, fluidly-moving limbs. Yes, unpredictability and improvisation were necessary in battle, but this went beyond that. This was total disassociation and disorganization. And, that all came back to—

"Second Commander Buird," I called him sharply, after adjourning the meeting.

Inexor approached me with worried wariness in his dark-blue eyes.

"My court-martial is on January seventh, in southeastern Nuria," I said, before he could even greet me. "I'm suspended from duty, until then."

"I know, Cease," he said, tone quiet and apologetic.

"And, I'm guilty."

He held his breath.

"I'll probably be discharged," I went on, "which would make you commander."

He blinked.

"But, I'm afraid I can't leave my fleet in your hands."

Inexor looked as though hit with a stun gun. "What are you saying?"

"I'm demoting you." I clasped my hands behind my back. "I don't know why it's taken me this long to do it. But, it's time I stopped waiting around, hoping you'll pull through. You've let me down, one too many times."

"But, Cease—"

"You're not to call me that again, soldier," I barked. "Dismissed."

Inexor didn't budge. "Who're you promoting?" he asked, voice low.

"I said, dismissed."

He kicked a chair. "Just tell me, Cease!"

There was a tense pause.

"Nurtic Leavesleft."

Inexor's jaw unhinged. "Leavesleft? But…he's—"

"A much better pilot, tactician and leader than you, despite a mere age of service—"

"He's Nurian!" Inexor threw his arms up over his head. "Nuria's the reason we're losing this war! You heard everyone, just now; almost all our battle casualties today were *Nurian.* How dare you turn your back on your own countrymen—"

"The way I see it, *you're* the one who turned your back on your men, when you threw them in the line of fire without any sort of strategy! Leavesleft will be commander and you'll replace him as officer of unit two."

"Who'll be his second?"

"That's for him to decide. And, you should be glad you still have any rank, at all. Now, get the hell out of my sight, before I change my mind!"

INEXOR BUIRD

So, that was what I got for standing beside Cease for over a decade and enduring nearly an age of captivity for saving his neck: rejection and demotion.

It took every ounce of discipline I had to face him at the pool, for spin-toss review. I hardly listened as he spoke, preoccupied with angry thoughts against him and Leavesleft. Not that Leavesleft did anything to me—he didn't even know about his promotion, yet—but, I hated him just the same. Him and his entire race for meddling in our war and weakening our military with their incompetence. There was no hope for Ichthyosis now, with a Nurian rookie as the Leader of the Resistance.

As pissed as I was at Cease, I would've given anything to see him cleared of his charges. I was afraid for Ichthyosis. Afraid of what would become of us without Cease's leadership.

I watched him pace back and forth now, speaking Nurian for the benefit of the newbies who 'graduated' from the Academy before learning two words of Ichthyothian. I wondered if they even understood him; his Nurian was accented and punctured with Ichthyothian words. Because Cease skipped so many grades growing up, he began learning Nurian a lot earlier in life than the rest of us. Because the human mind absorbed language better when younger, everyone expected Cease to have an easier time of it than his classmates. Wrong. When we met, he'd already failed first-level Nurian and was well on his way to botching it a second time. According to Cease's logs, Scarlet taught him some Conflagrian last July, for the infiltration. I wondered how they pulled *that* off without blowing their cover. Scarlet must've been one hell of a teacher, with the patience of a saint.

My attention got snagged now, by the sound of my name.

"In the water, Buird. You'll be my thrower and catcher," Cease ordered.

Seriously? I snapped on my helmet and plunked into the pool. After what *just* happened between us, he had the nerve to call me out for a demonstration. Why didn't he ask Leavesleft? Did pick me out of spite?

No. Cease had an attitude, but he wasn't vindictive or malicious. He probably picked me out of habit; he was used to turning to me for whatever he needed.

Cease slid into the water without a trace of a splash.

"Sloppy dive," his cold voice sounded in my helmet.

"You don't stop, do you?"

"Don't backtalk, soldier!"

"For someone who's suspended from duty, you sure are bossy," I shot acidly as we boosted in tandem off an underwater plank.

We broke the surface and I tossed him. He was light. Too light. I remembered him being substantially heavier, the last time we did this stunt together. So, he wound up flying a lot higher and further than I intended. I lunged, but my arms flailed and missed and he came crashing down on his shoulder. I dove after him and grabbed his collar but, apparently, he was already oriented and didn't need my help. He wrenched himself from my grasp and zipped to the surface far faster than I could follow.

Cease ordered me to the sidelines. I obliged, infuriated and thoroughly embarrassed. I expected him to call in someone else—Leavesleft, perhaps—but, instead, he dimmed the lights and activated the enormous, water-proof monitors on the far wall. Since returning home in July, I always wondered why one of the screens was cracked.

"Why's that one broken?" I whispered to Illia, standing beside me.

He smirked. "That happened a couple weeks before you came back. Scarlet didn't fasten her helmet properly before doing a demonstration, so it flew off of her head."

Hmm. Interesting. And, in five-plus months, Cease never thought to get it replaced?

"Computer, recall video number eight-seven-two-five-seven," Cease said to the wall. He looked back at us. "This is a *competent* performance of the spin-toss."

It was a video of him and Scarlet. Of course. I'd heard so much about Scarlet—not just from Cease, but everyone who served alongside her—but never actually saw her in action, until now. Flustered as I was, even I had to admit her agility was impressive. I'd never seen anyone dive like that before. She moved through the air and water like she was dancing.

While the video played a few times, Cease slumped in a corner of the dark room, resting his forehead on his folded knees. Never before had I seen Cease act so vulnerable, not even when we were kids. As I watched him sit there, looking so small and defeated, some of my anger toward him ebbed.

Cease was convinced his hallucinations were visions. And, that meant, he really believed the woman he loved burned alive.

When the video ended, Cease stood before his fleet and announced he'd been suspended from duty and wasn't sure if he'd be allowed back after his court-martial on January seventh.

The shock in the air was thick. The Ichthyothians stared at him, faces deadpan, while the Nurians looked at one another with open mouths.

"I'm appointing Nurtic Leavesleft as commander. Inexor Buird will fill the post of officer of unit two. Leavesleft is free to select his second commander." Cease gave Leavesleft a stern look. "Choose quickly, Leavesleft; these are dangerous times."

Leavesleft's eyes widened into hazel dinner-plates. The Nurians looked both pleased and alarmed while the Ichthyothians stared at their new commander with fiery ice. I imagined they regarded Scarlet—small, female, non-Ichthyothian—the same way, when Cease first promoted her.

And, with that, Cease dismissed us for his last time, thereby terminating the three-age reign of the greatest military leader in the history of Second Earth. When we left the pool, we were no longer the Nurro-Ichthyothian Diving Fleet, but a devastated, torn band of Nurians and Ichthyothians.

CEASE LECHATELIERITE

At thirty-six o'clock, Dr. Calibre and Nurse Raef came to my quarters and demanded I return to the hospital wing for further observation and treatment. Dizzy, nauseous and feverish, I let them take me.

I wasn't sure why, but as I lay awake in bed, listening to the beeps and ticks of the monitors all around me, I found myself thinking back to my very first sea battle.

At ten ages old and barely four feet in height, Commander Ecrof Ecreoc installed me as the officer of unit seven. I'd sped through the Academy faster than any diver before me, even my grandfather, Terminus, who won the First War. At fourteen, Inexor was the next youngest in the fleet, having graduated an age or two early. The rest ranged from fifteen to thirty.

Going into that battle, I didn't know how badly some of my comrades resented me for being promoted above them. Two men in their mid-twenties—Kerbma and Sutreppoc—devised a plot to end my life, accidentally-on-purpose.

On the back of every diving suit, where the collar joined the helmet in an airtight seal, there was a small 'lock/release' button, protected by four latches. Once properly fastened, the only way a diver's helmet could come off would be if all four latches were opened and the release-button were held down for two full seconds. Right before the battle, while I showered, Kerbma and Sutreppoc tampered with my helmet so it'd likely fall off while we were surface-riding. They anticipated I'd either drown, freeze to death or suffer skull implosion from water-pressure.

But, just before deploying, Commander Ecreoc suddenly and inexplicably reassigned me from surface-riding to diving from the overhead vitreous silica. Which meant my helmet flew off moments after I jumped from the shaft. I was sure to break the water feet-first and resurface as quickly as possible, but I still got frostbite all over my face and neck. Before hypothermia could kill me, I was taken aboard crystalline three.

The battle was a quick victory for Ichthyosis; we were all back to Icicle by nightfall. At about four o'clock the following morning, Kerbma and Sutreppoc dragged me from my bunk, naked, outside into the snow. Before Sutreppoc could stab me in the chest with an icicle, I kicked it out of his hand, breaking his fingers. Then, I jumped on Kerbma's back and strangled him to death. Sutreppoc, nursing his injury, fled the scene, hollering for Colonel Austere, leaving me alone with his friend's corpse, still warm in the snow.

Two weeks later, I was court-martialed. The jury called it self-defense and I got off, scot-free.

After that, no one dared target, tease or even talk to the ten-age-old officer. A period of intense alienation ensued— only Inexor, whom I'd met at age seven, spoke to me more often than business required. I became the most feared man in the fleet, besides the Commander himself.

It wasn't long before I figured out Ecreoc was aware of Kerbma and Sutreppoc's helmet-tampering scheme, all along. But, instead of directly intervening, he merely reassigned me from surface-riding to diving and sent me off to battle, ignorant and in imminent danger. That's when I realized I could trust no one. Not completely. Not even my commander. I really was alone in this war. The Conflagrians weren't my only enemy.

And, that was the day I truly hardened my heart to the world, becoming the fighting machine I needed to be.

INEXOR BUIRD

By mid-afternoon, Cease was marched out of Icicle in handcuffs and ushered aboard a police plane, bound for the Nurro-Ichthyothian Military Prison in Alcove City. The media pounced on him the moment he set foot on Nurian soil, at night; the fleet watched it all unfold on live television in the rec room. Lights flashed as reporters shouted questions and brandished microphones. Cease ignored them all as he walked, eyes hidden behind his reflective visual band. All the while, the voice of a Channel Seven reporter rambled on about his charges, apparent signs of 'mental instability' and, of course, how he'd inaccurately declared victory, back in August.

About ten minutes into the broadcast, 'Commander' Nurtic Leavesleft barged in and turned off the television.

"We shouldn't pay any attention to that media hype," he said. "It's not respectful to our commander."

I thought it ridiculous Leavesleft insisted on calling Cease 'our commander' when the man was suspended from duty and hauled off to jail. Was that Leavesleft's idea of forging intra-fleet unity? I also noticed he addressed us in Ichthyothian, though many of the greener rookies hardly knew two words of the language.

Leavesleft ushered me out into the hallway and closed the door behind us. Immediately, I heard the TV turn back on. If Cease were the one who forbade us from watching it, it'd stay off for eternity.

"What is it?" I snapped.

He didn't reprimand me for my tone, as Cease would've. He held out his right hand and gave me a big, dimpled grin, as though we were lifelong buddies.

"Congratulations, Buird, I've decided to make you my second-in-command. My old sub-leader, Wodahs Vestige, will take unit two and appoint his own sub."

I didn't shake his hand. "What's this, a pity promotion?"

Leavesleft shook his head. "Not at all, sir. You deserve it."

"Really?"

"Well, everyone deserves a second chance."

Ugh. Nurians were always saying such stupid, sentimental things. What did that even mean? No, everyone did not deserve a second chance. The System sure didn't. Neither did unapologetic, sexual predators like Amok Kempt. Nor murderous traitors like Kerbma and Sutreppoc. Would Leavesleft give any of them a second chance? I doubted it.

"The fleet needs an Ichthyothian in a top leadership position," he babbled on, "and who better to fill that post than the man who's worked closest with our commander for—"

"Oh, so you're promoting me to look fair in front of everybody," I shot, "so the Ichthyothians will stop hating you. Is that it?"

Leavesleft blinked. "Sir, I understand you're upset over what just happened to our commander; we all are. But, there's no reason to take out your frustrations on me—"

"You understand *nothing*, Nurian!" I burst, throwing him a punch.

But, before my blow could land, he caught my fist tightly in his left hand.

"I won't tolerate insubordination." All the warmth was gone from his hazel eyes and his voice, usually so mellow, was hard. "Because, like it or not, I *am* your commander now, so you better show me some respect. Understood?"

There was a tense silence.

"Yes, sir."

He released his iron grip.

"I'm still offering you the position," he said, stiffly. "And, if you don't want it, I have other candidates in mind. So, quit wasting my time and take it or leave it, right now."

I exhaled through my nose. "I'll take it."

Leavesleft's face broke out into its usual smile. "Great!" he said, completely himself again. "See you tomorrow morning!"

And, he walked away with a spring in his step, leaving me alone in the dark corridor.

SCARLET JULY

Unable to fall sleep, I slipped outside to walk the sandy shore of the Fervor Sea, breathing the humid air with an open mouth. The deep, brown night sky was cluttered with black clouds, floating like slime in a muddy stream. Alpha and Omega, the two moons, illuminated the waves lapping the beach. Somewhere in the water's depths, an active fragment of the Core Crystal lay like a sleeping dragon, yet to unleash its terror on an unsuspecting Second Earth. I closed my moist eyes and imagined I was soaring thousands of miles across the three seas, littered with the debris of countless battles, to the North Ichthyosis Island—the nation to which all my thoughts eventually led.

I heard a rustle in the trees behind me. I turned and saw Ambrek creeping along, sturdy figure like an animated, copper sculpture. He blew out his torch with a single puff, wispy smoke curling around his bronze face. He was almost to the cabin's side door before he noticed me.

"Scarlet!" he breathed, surprised. He tossed his extinguished post to the sand and ran to me like we hadn't seen each other in months. "What're you doing, out here?"

I shrugged. "Can't sleep."

"Yeah, me neither," he said. "Went for a walk."

"Don't get kidnapped again," I joked, lamely. I attempted a smile, and a few tears squeezed out the corners of my eyes. As I quickly wiped them away, my right sleeve flopped back to my elbow, revealing the wound on my forearm.

Ambrek gasped. "What happened, here?" He took my tiny arm in his large, muscular hands.

"Got hit by an arrow, during the battle you missed yesterday. I didn't think to heal it when my aura crystallized for a moment. I was a little…overwhelmed."

And, now that I was thinking about it, it really did hurt. A lot. The pain shot all the way to my shoulder.

Ambrek ducked into the cabin for a moment and returned, pail in hand. He rinsed my stinging arm and wrapped it in his handkerchief. Scarlet blood seeped into the copper-green cloth, forming grotesque brown spots.

"You can't ignore stuff like that, Scarlet. You've got to look after yourself. Or, at least, let me look after you."

I didn't answer. I just gazed at the sea and tried to swallow the lump in my throat. Ambrek stood behind me and began to massage my tense shoulders with his strong fingertips. Muscles slowly relaxing, I soon found myself leaning back against him, his bulky arms nestled tightly around my waist.

Ambrek sacrificed a lot for the revolution. He left his family in Ardor Village and came to Red Headquarters in the northern region of the island to commit himself to the rebellion and to me, selflessly and professionally putting aside all vindictiveness he could've harbored upon learning which Ichthyothian soldier killed his sister in combat. He understood Cease was only doing his job, and Crimson—under the influence of the Core Crystal—was doing hers. Ambrek reminded me of my fifteen-age-old self who went great lengths to become a diver just to find Cease in particular and become his secret weapon against the System.

I closed my burning eyes and allowed Ambrek to fully support my weight. It was good to know I had at least one solid rock in my crazy world, one person I could always count on.

I grew sleepier as time passed. Ambrek turned me around. His eyes looked orange in Alpha and Omega's eerie, reddish glow. He stroked my hair, my jaw, my neck.

"Ambrek?" I murmured, feeling a prickle of confusion mingled with fear. His hands felt so good on me, his touch so gentle yet masculine.

"Scarlet," he whispered, leaning in. And, he kissed me hard on the mouth, powerful arms encircling me.

Well, that sure woke me up. Helpless to break free of his impervious hold, all I could do to deflect his warm, insistent lips was turn my head.

"No, Ambrek, we can't," I panted, tear-soaked cheek against his broad chest.

This wasn't happening. I couldn't afford for things to get weird between us. Ambrek was too important to the revolution. Too important to me. I couldn't lose him. I needed him. But, not like this.

Not yet.

Ambrek's arms stiffened around my body. "Why not?"

What could I say? Because I was still hung up on my ex-commander whom I'd likely never see again? A man I knew for a mere two months and hadn't spoken to in almost five? A man whose memory only waned as those months passed and I spent every waking minute serving side-by-side with Ambrek—kind, strong, brave Ambrek— who left his whole world behind, just for me. Ambrek, who was right here, in Conflagria, to stay.

"It's because of him, isn't it," Ambrek grunted.

Lids scrunched shut, I only nodded.

"Scarlet," he said, voice heavy, "you're never going to see him again. When you left Ichthyosis, your relationship—if you can even call what you had a relationship—ended. It's been over since August. It's almost January. There's nothing to stay faithful to."

I swallowed. "I know."

"And, I want to be there for you."

"Y-you already are and have been, Ambrek," I choked. "You've b-been nothing but good to me, since you came around." Good. What an understatement. "I'm just not ready, yet."

"Yet," he echoed.

I was silent. It felt traitorous to even think that Ambrek stood a chance of ever winning my heart. But, after months of suppressing the thought, I had no choice but to ask myself, now: would I've fallen for him, if I never met Cease? *Could* I still fall for him, once my memory of Cease faded enough?

My heart thudded against my ribcage as I realized the answer to both questions was yes.

"Scarlet, I've been meaning to tell you something." He squeezed my shoulders. "Scarlet, please look at me."

I hesitated, then met his sad stare.

"I love you," he said, gold gaze boring through me. "I have for a while. And, I think all our comrades have figured that out, by now. Except you."

There was a long, painful pause during which neither of us blinked nor breathed.

"Ambrek," I finally piped. "You know I love you, too. You're the best thing that's happened to me since coming home."

His lips parted.

"But, I'm *in* love with Cease. Still. It's just…different."

He closed his mouth, and his eyes.

"I'm so sorry." My voice cracked. "It's too soon for me. I know everything you said is true—he and I aren't together anymore and never will be—but, I just can't logic away my feelings for him. It doesn't work like that. I need more time."

He nodded, chest rising and falling.

"Ambrek, I don't want this to come between us—between our friendship and our work," I whimpered. "I can't lose you, too."

He opened his eyes, and they were wet. "You won't," he said, softly. "Because there's nothing you could do to scare me away. No matter what, I'll always stand by you. And, I'll respect your healing process. Just, please, let me know when the cuts have scabbed over, okay?"

Overcome by relief and exhaustion and gratitude, I let him envelop me in his arms, one last time.

"Thank you," I cried into his chest, wondering what I did to deserve such an incredible friend and comrade.

CEASE LECHATELIERITE

Flanked by security, I was handcuffed and taken aboard a police plane. My court-martial was scheduled for January seventh in a Nurian military courthouse, since all courts on Ichthyothian soil were booked until May and the Trilateral Committee wasn't keen to keep the Leader of the Ichthyothian Resistance locked up for five months without a formal sentence. Until January seventh, I would be detained in a prison in Alcove City.

At some point during the flight, I fell asleep. I awoke to the sight of flames, nearly licking my face. I blinked. There was a torch in my left hand. My right was outstretched, pushing aside low-hanging tree branches as I padded, barefoot, across the coarse, warm sand, heading toward an old, wooden cabin. Blowing out the flames with a single puff, I reached into the smoky darkness for a doorknob. But, then, I felt the nagging sensation I was being watched. I looked toward the beach and my heart stopped.

A pair of glassy, green eyes stared back at me from a sad, flushed face, framed by wiry, shoulder-length, red hair.

"Scarlet!" I breathed.

She was alive! Alive and well and standing right in front of me! Somehow, we were no longer separated by thousands of miles. Somehow, she must've survived a fiery torch to the head. I wished I could let all my men know she was okay. I dropped my post and ran to her, an incomprehensible mash of vowels escaping my lips. She replied to me with a similar-sounding garble. Why were we speaking Conflagrian instead of Ichthyothian or Nurian? How did I know the words to say? Wait, what *was* I saying?

I stopped caring about words and languages when Scarlet leaned her body against mine, hair blowing back in the sea-breeze, tickling my chin and neck, filling my nostrils with her wood-smoke scent. A strange mix of happiness and anguish welled in my chest as I turned her tiny, trembling figure in my arms and kissed her, hard, on the lips.

Scarlet squirmed and turned her head, whispering something as she pressed her wet cheek to my chest. I looked down, and my eyes fell on the half-empty pail at our feet. I caught sight of my own reflection in the water, and a tanned face with gold eyes, a square jaw and spiky, copper hair stared back at me. I gasped; this was the same face I saw in the tinted helmet of Ecivon Wen, after I snapped his neck with my fingers.

The land jerked beneath my feet. I opened my eyes—a strange thing to do when I thought they were already open. A Nurian voice came on the intercom, alerting us of our arrival in Alcove City. I breathed with an open mouth, blinking at the rain-spotted window. Alcove City. Not a Conflagrian beach. I was aboard a police plane that just touched down on the tarmac. I wasn't gazing at the moonlit Fervor Sea, holding Scarlet July in my arms.

Scarlet July. Anxiety, anger and confusion overcame me, in an instant. I closed my eyes and bowed my head. I wanted to scream. I wanted to cry. I wanted to vomit. I wanted to kill something. I didn't understand why or how, but she'd been turned. She was a System supporter, now. That was the obvious explanation for what I just saw. She wasn't a prisoner-of-war; she wasn't held against her will. She embraced the amber-eyed, System pilot lovingly. She let him kiss her. I trembled. Scarlet was a traitor. She betrayed her people. She betrayed the revolution. She betrayed the alliance.

She betrayed me.

No. How could it be? I gnawed the inside of my cheek until it bled. Was the vision proof enough? Was there more to what I saw? Was there any doubt I could give her the benefit of? My heart hammered in the region of my Adam's apple, anger eating away at my insides like lava from the Fire Pit. If I ever saw Scarlet face-to-face and confirmed that she was, in fact, an enemy of Ichthyosis, I knew what I had to do. It'd be duty first; I'd destroy her.

* * *

Morning came, and I was thrown in a sticky, smelly, overcrowded cell. Sweaty faces gaped openly at me as I entered—of course, they all recognized the Leader of the Ichthyothian Resistance. Many of them even stood back or stepped aside, intimidated despite the several inches and pounds they had on me.

"Watch out, he's in practice," someone said.

"Commander Lechatelierite?" a voice called, to my left.

I turned and saw the stocky figure and narrow, mud-brown eyes of Amok Kempt. My old second-in-command. The man who tried to rape Scarlet July on her sixteenth birthday.

I was already in a foul mood, and the presence of Amok Kempt wasn't exactly helping.

"Amok," I said through tight lips.

Everyone seemed excited I recognized someone. They watched attentively as Amok and I stood, a couple yards apart, sizing each other up. I guessed this was the closest thing the inmates had to entertainment in here, aside from the monotonous, thirty-six-hour-a-day news, playing on a little, fuzzy, far-outdated television in the corner of the cell.

"How the mighty have fallen." Amok's eyes were full of vengeful laughter. "Good to see you again."

"Wish I could say the same," I answered, coolly.

His gaze hovered on my pant hems, dragging on the floor. "Looking a little sickly there, *sir*," he said the last word teasingly, mockingly. "What, did Icicle send you over 'cause they can't afford to feed their men anymore?"

I just saw Scarlet swap spit with a System soldier; I was in no mood to be goaded by the bastard who molested her in the showers.

"That's a lot of trash talk for an iced diver whose ass got kicked by an eighty-pound girl in the locker-room," I sneered. "Ran away from her screaming, isn't that right?"

At this, the crowd went wild. Amok's cheeks reddened.

"This is Channel Seven," a blonde anchorwoman spoke in rapid Nurian, on TV. "I'm Claver Causerie, reporting live from the nation's capital. Our top story this morning is the arrest of the eighteen-age-old Leader of the Nurro-Ichthyothian Resistance, Cease Terminus Lechatelierite." The screen displayed a close-up of my banded face as I was marched out of the plane in handcuffs, last night. "The Diving Commander, who inaccurately declared victory in the war five months ago, has been suspended from duty on three charges, and will be detained in the Alcove City Military Prison until his court-martial on January seventh of the ninety-fourth age. The suspect's charges include: violating the Geneva Convention, commanding an unauthorized attack on Conflagrian soil and permitting a Conflagrian mage to serve in the Diving Fleet."

The broadcast displayed Insouci Raef with a swarthy, brunette reporter in a tight black dress. The words 'LIVE EXCLUSIVE' flashed across the bottom of the screen.

"This is Rethy Swa, reporting live from the Icicle Diving Base in Aventurine City, North Ichthyosis. I'm with

Mrs. Insouci Rorret Raef, a nurse on the medical team that was responsible for the Commander's care."

She held a comically-large microphone to the nurse's face. Raef, dressed in baggy, white scrubs with her platinum-blonde hair in a sloppy bun, looked at the camera with discomfort in her sapphire-blue eyes.

"Commander Lechatelierite had a heatstroke earlier this week, during a conference at the Nurian Diving Academy, immediately falling into a coma. Upon waking, he had a seizure. Dr. Calibre and I believe he's also suffering from post-traumatic stress disorder."

"Is it true the suspect assaulted you?" Swa asked in a juicy, scandalized tone, apparently uninterested in my array of medical problems.

"W-well, he didn't know what he was doing," Raef replied, a fearful edge to her voice. "He was unconscious at the time."

"Would you be willing to share with our viewers exactly how he attacked you?"

Raef tucked a stray wisp of pale hair behind her ear. "Um, he struck me in the jaw and, um, tried to strangle me, I think."

"You *think?*" The reporter's eyes widened in dramatized shock. "Do you plan to press charges?"

"N-no," she sputtered. "Like I said, he was unconscious. He wasn't in control of himself. He was responding to a hallucination."

"Thank you, Mrs. Raef."

The nurse looked relieved to be dismissed.

The reporter flashed her white smile at the camera. "We're also privileged with the opportunity to speak with the Ichthyothian Diving Colonel Autoero Augustus Austere, the officer who oversaw the young Commander's progression through the Childhood Program." Austere came into view.

"Colonel, there's been talk of PTSD, hallucinations and violent outbursts. You've worked closely with the suspect since his birth. When did all this start? Could mental instability be the reason he so flagrantly disregarded the law?"

Austere's icy eyes were set. "I believe Commander Lechatelierite had full possession of his mental faculties when committing the alleged war-crimes. He didn't start showing signs of post-traumatic stress disorder until August."

Swa raised an angular eyebrow. "So, the suspect's mental health has never been called into question before then, sir?"

"Eight ages ago, he was tried for killing one of his comrades and injuring another. But, the court ruled his actions as self-defense."

Swa made a big show of gaping at the camera. "So, the suspect was only ten, at the time?"

"Yes."

"Thank you for your time, Colonel."

He nodded curtly and stepped out of view.

The blonde anchorwoman returned to the screen. "The suspect appointed one of our own, from the nation's capital—twenty-age-old Nurtic Ehud Leavesleft—in his place. Commander Leavesleft has agreed to share a few words with us."

Leavesleft apparently didn't appear live; they cut to a clip of him standing in a different room, alone. He looked at the camera, hazel gaze profound.

"Commander Lechatelierite is a war-hero who gave the alliance everything he had. Serving under him was a true honor. I'd die for him. I'm sure every man in this fleet would do the same. Taking him away was a big mistake."

And, Leavesleft's 'interview' was over. I immediately understood why Channel Seven didn't let him talk live—they wanted to cut his footage down to a tiny sliver, because what he had to say was positive. The station probably only allowed him to speak for the purpose of feigning some measure of neutrality. They couldn't be too obvious about their bias and have *all* their interviewees smear me.

"The Diving Fleet's Second Commander—twenty-two-age-old, base-raised Inexor Adaman Buird—has also agreed to comment on camera."

Again, they cut to a clip. So, I guessed Inexor was also about to come to my defense.

His angry face filled the screen. He spoke in rapid Ichthyothian, which the station subtitled in Nurian. A few of his words had to be censored with beeps: "Cease Lechatelierite was the best d— military leader Ichthyosis has ever seen! You pieces of s— just wrote your death sentence by removing him from command! Those ingrate sons of b— who took him away are going to be f— sorry when the entire war crumbles on their f— ingrate heads!"

The blonde anchorwoman returned, ready to discredit Inexor completely: "Inexor Buird served as acting commander throughout the suspect's coma during which he led the Diving Fleet into a crushing defeat against the Water Forces of the South Conflagrablaze Captive, failing to prevent the System from ransacking the ports of Alcove City and getting away with half a dozen submarines. Channel Seven will keep you updated on the unfolding court-martial of Commander Cease Lechatelierite." She paused. "In other news…"

My fellow inmates stared at me, a buzz spreading across the cell.

"Hallucinations?"

"The Commander cracked!"

"Kamikaze crazy."

"Wait, he killed a comrade at *ten?*"

"Better watch it, fellas."

"He don't look big enough to squash a flea."

"...At the Nurian Trade Centerscraper in southeast Alcove City," the anchor was saying, "where the Ichthyothian-born CEO of the Nurro-Ichthyothian Underwater Vessel Manufacturing Company, Mr. Finis Arrete Lechatelierite, expressed his concern regarding the increasing number of thefts from the ports..."

Wait, what about my father? It was hard to hear over all the chatter.

"SILENCE!" I erupted, and magically, everyone obeyed.

"Channel Seven dispatched a team to the Centerscraper earlier this morning to capture Mr. Finis Lechatelierite's address."

The TV then displayed my father, flanked by microphones and lit by countless camera flashes as he stood in front of a sea of black and charcoal suits. His stony, grey eyes didn't dare blink.

"Nuria has outfitted the Ichthyothian Military at a great cost to itself; we demand they fulfill their obligation to the alliance and protect our ports from further harm," he fumed. "Commander Nurtic Leavesleft, I'm talking to you."

I looked away. Everything was going wrong. Everything. The alliance hung me out to dry. Nuria and Ichthyosis were cleaving apart. The spectral web was crystallizing out of nowhere. And, somehow, someway, Scarlet July turned her back on the Red Revolution.

And, on me.

Amok looked me in the eye and laughed. His laugh was deep and throaty. A few of the others joined in. Heat rose to my face. I strode forward, grabbed the front of Amok's orange uniform and threw him backward into the television set; broken glass rained everywhere. The cell went dead quiet.

SCARLET JULY

I threw myself under the stone staircase and aimed at the System warriors scurrying past. Pulling my bow's taut cord to my chin, I squinted down a long, wooden arrow. After a lifetime of spectral eyesight and nine months fighting with fantastic Ichthyothian weaponry, it felt clumsy to wage war with bows, arrows and swords while half-blind with twenty-twenty vision.

I hit four men in succession. Cover blown now, I had no choice but to abandon my hiding place. I ran up the sweeping stairs, three enemies hot on my tail.

My job in this skirmish was to serve as a distraction, while my co-leaders and a handful of other Reds moved in on the System's stolen crafts. For the third time in only a couple days, we were raiding the Ardor Village Water Forces Base—better known as the Mage Castle, whose hangar was located along the Fervor River—endeavoring to steal a sub we'd use to scour the Briny Ocean for the fragment of the Core Crystal. Our first two tries were a total bust, but perhaps the third time would be the charm?

Below, I saw Ambrek, Fair and the others barrel toward the nearest parked vessel—a convertible sub-plane—firing arrows and swinging swords. But, a System warrior got to it before they did. He jumped into the cockpit, hovered a few feet off the ground, swiveled around and opened fire.

Our primitive weapons were no match for a Nordic fighter. Immediately, the Reds scattered, abandoning their advance.

The ship tilted its nose up and fired in my direction. The stone steps below me exploded, stranding me on the top tiers with three men who wanted to kill me. I retrieved a coil of Ichthyothian deadline from under my swathe and lassoed the crystal chandelier. At times like these, I was glad I didn't weigh much. I leapt before the smoke could clear, vanishing from my pursuers' sights. In the midst of the mushroom cloud, I let go, landed on the hardwood floor with a roll, jumped to my feet and hightailed out the door and into the night.

Coughing, I ran into the forest, untied my scabrous, mounted it and galloped all the way back to Headquarters. My breath caught in my chest when I went inside and saw Ambrek on the floor, a diagonal slash running all the way from his left palm to his elbow. I dropped to my knees and took his large, muscular forearm in my hands. I pressed his sleeve against the sword wound, to help stop the bleeding.

"Fair, get some water, rubbing alcohol and towels."

Fair nodded, scurried off, and returned a couple minutes later with the supplies. Ambrek scrunched his eyes shut and bit his lip as I cleansed and wrapped his arm.

"That was the most pointless battle yet!" Fair spat as she paced about. "We infiltrated the Mage Castle three times in a row. Three times! And, for what? To run away bleeding?" She gestured to Ambrek.

"I'm fine!" he hollered a little too loudly, obviously trying to disguise a cry of agony. Heart wrenching at the sound, I put my arms around him.

"All this, to try to steal a ship the alliance should've just given us, in the first place," Fair growled. "I find it hard to believe they can't spare one lousy scout."

"Knowing how the Nordic world thinks of us, I can believe it," I said, dryly. "It's not that they can't afford it, it's that they still don't trust us *fire-savages*, even after everything we've done for them. Racism is alive and well on Second Earth. Moreover, most Nordics don't understand the distinction between the System and the rest of us. They see all of Conflagria as *them*. The enemy."

"You said your boyfriend understands," Fair spat. I felt Ambrek's muscles tighten under my touch. "Why doesn't Cease just screw the alliance and give us one of his ships, himself?"

"Cease isn't her boyfriend," Ambrek croaked.

"I-I'm sure he wants to," I sputtered. I knew Cease; if there was anything he could do to help me, he'd do it, without question. Physical impossibility or complete ignorance of my need would be the only things that'd stop him. "His hands must be tied, in some way. He may not even know we asked. The Alliance and the Trilateral Committees consider him a 'mage sympathizer,' after all. They either didn't tell him about your letter or they're doing everything in their power to stop him from taking action."

"Quit making excuses for him already and just admit he's no different than the rest of his kind," Fair seethed. "Nordic elitist bastards, all of them."

Heat rushed to my face. I opened my mouth, but Ambrek spoke before I could.

"So, we obviously have to try something else, to get a ship. We can't sit around and wait for Cease to save the day, and we can't keep attacking the Mage Castle, to no end."

"You got any better ideas?" Fair snapped.

"As a matter of fact, I do. When I was kidnapped, I saw a sea battle, and that got me thinking," he began.

I always thought it strange Ambrek was held hostage on a sub. That'd only make sense if he were captured at sea. Why drag him from Headquarters all the way out to the water? I didn't understand the System's methods, at all. I couldn't imagine Cease doing such a thing.

"I watched the Water Forces in action and they're really disorganized," Ambrek went on.

"Ain't that the truth," Fair murmured. She used to be the Leader of Flame Team Seven, before the diffusion.

"So, I don't think it'd be too hard to kidnap a pilot and co-pilot as they're prepping for dispatch, steal their suits and secretly take their place. We'd deploy, undercover. Then, we'd sever our intercom, making it look like a tech error, and slip away from the battle to search for the crystal."

Fair and I stared.

"That's a bit…far-fetched, isn't it?" Fair gaped. "I've never heard of a plan where so many things could go wrong."

Ambrek shrugged. "Well, these are just my spontaneous musings. Clearly, we'll need to think things through a lot more, before taking action."

He came up with all that, right now?

"Slip away," Fair echoed. "Maybe the System would be too blind to realize what we're up to, but the Ichthyothians would sure notice an enemy sub trying to sneak off. Ichthyothians are an alert people. If I tried to pull anything like that when I was in the Water Forces, half a dozen crystallines would be on my tail in about ten seconds. Ichthyothians are always aware of their surroundings."

"Sure, *Ichthyothians* may be." Ambrek smiled. "But, you're forgetting something: Scarlet said most of the Diving Fleet are Nurian, now. From what I saw, we could probably dance naked on their crystallines and they wouldn't notice."

Was it just me, or did Ambrek sound a little *too* happy about the fleet's mediocrity? I glared.

"Nothing against Cease, of course!" he added quickly. "All I'm saying is, their fleet's underperformance can be used to our advantage."

"I have a safer idea," I said. Ambrek's plan wasn't just unsafe, it was totally nuts. Maybe some of that rubbing alcohol got into his bloodstream and went to his head. "Let's contact a Nurian ship manufacturer and ask them to loan us a scout."

Ambrek sighed. "Scarlet, we already made a plea to the Alliance Committee and their reply was the most insulting thing I've read in my life."

"Then, we won't ask the Alliance Committee and we won't just send a stupid letter that'll take forever to get there only to be tossed in a recycling bin by an intern. Let's go to the manufacturers directly, at the Nurian Trade Centerscraper. They could surely afford to loan us a couple suits and a single craft. And, they're less likely to refuse if we ask right to their faces."

"How would we even get there?" Ambrek sounded uncharacteristically irritated. "We obviously don't have a ship—that's the whole reason we're stuck in this mess."

I ran a hand through my wiry hair, fingers snagging kinks. "Well, we don't have to have a ship. We don't have to go by sea, at all. We could fly."

"Sure, let's just hop onto the plane we *don't* have," he grumbled.

I gave him a playful shove. "Come on, Ambrek. Now, *you're* the one thinking like a Nordic. We don't have to use technology, at all. We could just ride a pine dragon to the city."

He gawked at me. "Ride a dragon across the sea? That's crazy."

"It's less crazy than kidnapping System soldiers and throwing ourselves in the middle of a raging, sea battle," Fair retorted.

Ambrek cupped his square jaw in his huge palm. "Well, if we're going to fly all the way out there, why bother haggling with Nurian businessmen? Why not just snag a ship from the ports ourselves?"

"*Snag* a ship?" I looked at Ambrek in disbelief. "You mean, steal?"

He shrugged. "Yeah, whatever."

"Ambrek, we can't steal from Nordics."

He folded his massive arms across his broad chest. "Why not? The System does it all the time."

I couldn't believe my ears. What kind of justification was that? The System also brainwashed generations and routinely executed the weak and elderly.

"Exactly. We're not the System. We won't stoop to their level. The Nordics are our friends."

Fair snorted.

"But, Scarlet, we'd be doing it to save Conflagria and the Nurro-Ichthyothian Alliance," Ambrek grumbled. "What difference does it make, how we get the job done?"

This wasn't the Ambrek I knew and loved. What on Tincture's island was wrong with him? Was it just the injury talking?

I looked him in the eye. "It makes all the difference. Ends don't justify means, Ambrek. Not even in war."

FINIS LECHATELIERITE

I stroked my moustache, poring over the business section of the *Alcove City Post*. The ongoing Conflagrian theft was taking a serious toll on the Nurian economy, not to mention my company. And, whatever affected Nuria, affected Ichthyosis.

I tossed the paper on my desk and turned to the grand window behind me. I gazed out at the bustling streets and wondered if this city could ever start to feel like home. My wife, Qui, hated it here, too—more than me, if that was possible.

We'd been here for about an age now, during which we only went home once, four months ago. Work hardly let us get away, these days. Our trip was brief and the purpose was to see Cease. It was the first time the Trilateral Committee permitted us to interact with him since his birth. Our visit was a reward to him, for having 'won' the war.

I remembered the anxiety that assaulted my stomach when we traveled to Icicle Base on that windy, August day. I remembered the excitement and fear that overcame me as a young officer named Nurtic Leavesleft lead us down a winding, narrow corridor and asked Illia Frappe to alert the Admiral he had guests. And, the disbelief and awe that welled in my chest when, at long last, Qui and I saw our small-statured son approach, staring at us with those eyes that were so much like my own, narrow face framed by a heavy mop of his mother's dark hair. Cease didn't merely look at you—he gazed intently, blinks few and far between.

His steely eyes and thin, tight lips revealed nothing but mild surprise as he greeted us. We were only permitted to stay with him for thirty minutes—thirty minutes after seventeen ages of separation—during which he never relaxed.

During those seventeen ages, Qui and I diligently followed all news stories on the Second War and watched every documentary we could find on the Ichthyothian military. Some of the documentaries devoted a portion to the life and genius of the Resistance Leader. Those images were all we got to see of our son as he grew up.

The Trilateral Committee sent us letters every now and then, relaying in few words the important steps Cease took in his career. At ten, he became the youngest soldier in the history of Icicle Diving Academy to graduate into the fleet. He was promoted from unit leader to commander, within five ages. Qui and I were proud, but worried sick. Qui asked me daily, what if Cease died in battle today? What if he died without knowing he had a family who loved and wanted him? We always wondered what Cease thought of us, if he ever did. Was he angry? Did he resent us? Did he think we let him go willingly? Did he believe he was abandoned, thrown away? Did he know the Trilateral Committee left us no choice? Qui would cry to me: why didn't the TC just depend on adult enlistments?

I knew the TC's argument. While they never fully relied on voluntary adult enlistments, they did try to supplement the troops by allowing it for a few ages, back when I was a teen. And, in the end, they claimed these civilian-raised soldiers turned out to be disappointments, more often than not. They ultimately determined there was no point to acquiring adult Ichthyothians since they already found all suitable candidates as kids. If these adult wannabees weren't capable back then, they wouldn't be now, the theory went. Currently, adult enlistments were only open to Nurians, since Nuria didn't have a childhood screening process. Not to mention, Nuria was massive and had plenty of so-called 'disposable manpower,' whereas Ichthyosis was too small to deplete its young, male population for no gain.

When I was born, I was also taken from my mother, Christallina Aveline, and my father, Terminus Expiri Lechatelierite, the Diving Captain who managed to win the First War despite minor proportionate-dwarfism and left-eye blindness. With perfect vision and no trace of any developmental disorders, I got iced after only three ages at the academy, because I was 'lacking in reflexive capability and intellectual capacity,' the official discharge report stated. My father was angry and ashamed. He took my failure as a personal offense, reminding me often that I dishonored the family name and would never amount to anything.

Growing up, I was neither an honor roll student nor a star athlete. I was an average kid with no outstanding talents. My father's constant put-downs and reprimands killed my motivation and confidence. Essentially, I was a nothing because, since I was iced from Icicle, I was told that was all I could be.

And then, the morning of December twenty-second of the forty-seventh age, when I was seven, my father did something he never dared before: sought to spend time with me. He wanted to take me to work. Salmon fishing, abalone fishing and oil mining were the three thriving industries in Ichthyosis. Salmon, pearls and petroleum mostly sustained Ichthyosis's trade relations with Nuria. My father's post-military career was the commercial fishing industry.

I was thrilled to tag along for a day, not to mention, quite eager to please. This was my golden chance to finally show him I was a son worth paying attention to and, who knew, maybe a future business partner. My nerves hammered as he took me aboard a massive ship.

"Not too different from a vitreous silica," he said, clapping my shoulder for the first time I could remember. "Except, we carry scouts called 'sparks' instead of crystallines."

That morning, I watched, fascinated, as our ship lugged enormous cable nets, filled with salmon. I found myself intrigued by the structure and functioning of the ships. Towing everything on one side seemed kind of dumb and inefficient. Why not build stern trawlers that could tow over a ramp, instead? Or, maybe, hang nets from booms on both sides? That'd increase the hauling rate. A lot. I smiled to myself as I daydreamed about revolutionizing the entire industry, winning not only fame and fortune but my father's love.

Typically, I was shy to voice my thoughts to him because he was so firmly convinced of my stupidity. But, his willingness to take me to work that day gave me unusual courage. So, I marched right up to the navigation and hydraulic panel where he and some of his coworkers sat and told them all about my ideas. As I spoke, my father watched me with his ever-alert right eye, his cloudy left one staunchly fixed forward. I always wondered what caused the terrible scar that stretched all the way from his pupil to the tip of his sharp jaw. He never shared the story with me, but I assumed it was a wound from the war.

"So, instead of towing the trawl nets from one side," I said, "you could have a stern ramp, or maybe booms swinging out on *both* sides," I gestured excitedly, right hand knocking the double-cable-release button. At once, the powerblock discharged all its nets and salmon spilled out into the sea like silver confetti.

My father grabbed my collar and dragged me from the bridge, growling, "You're never coming anywhere with me, again! You're a fool who'll never amount to anything—a disgrace to the family name! I'd impale myself on a reef before letting my company pass to your hands! You'd be a failure at business, just as you were at diving!"

"Captain," a female voice issued from down the hall, "your spark is ready for—" The woman stopped dead in the doorway. "Is everything alright, sir?"

"Of course." He let go of my collar. "I was just telling Finis he's welcome to come out on my spark to watch me scuba-dive for abalone," he said, voice monotonous.

She smiled. "Aw, doesn't that sound fun, Finis?" she asked in a cutesy voice. "You'll get to catch a glimpse of what daddy did in the fleet! He was a great diver, you know."

"Yes, I know," I said sadly, looking down at my shoes.

After that, my father had no choice but to take me with him.

"Touch nothing," he ordered menacingly, as we boarded. He looked so small and thin in his skintight scuba-suit, yet no less frightening to me.

"Yes, papa."

I gawked at the glittering console, imagining we were inside a crystalline warship instead of a fishing spark. My father piloted us to the bottom of the cobalt-blue sea, beautifully encrusted with frosty coral. After about half an hour, we passed an ugly heap of grey and black rubble.

"Papa, what's that?" I gasped.

"Looks to me like debris from the war." He gestured to the co-pilot's joystick that I was expressly forbidden to touch. "All my ships are equipped with minimal weapons systems, just in case we come across a mage still holding a grudge."

He anchored the spark and dove into the water, elegantly streamlining toward the coral. I sighed, thinking about my expulsion from the Childhood Program. I didn't remember a thing from my time at Icicle, but I wished I did. It would've been amazing to be a part of the Diving Fleet, piloting ships like this and diving gracefully through the water, defending my country and bringing honor to my family.

Papa would've been so proud.

It took him a while to gather seven cases of abalone. But, I wasn't bored as I sat on my hands in the co-pilot's seat and admired his mercury movements. Soon, my sad thoughts gave way to flying fantasies, as I fingered the controls before me. I imaged I was a diving officer, dexterously navigating a crystalline, giving rapid-fire orders to my subordinates and shooting down every colorful Conflagrian craft in my path.

I gently touched the joystick and yelled, "Ka-POW! I've got another dragon ship!" My thumb grazed the green button. "I'm tailing another one! FIRE!"

Before I could stop myself, I actually pressed the button; a beam emitted from the front of the spark. I gasped, horrified, as light engulfed the windshield. Papa was going to be so mad! He was going to beat me to a pulp when he came back and, this time, no one would be around to stop him. I put my hands over my face as I waited for him, frozen in my seat like a shackled POW.

Long moments passed and he didn't return. I heard a knocking sound so I peeked through my fingers to see what it was. Abalone shells were colliding into the windshield. How strange. Abalone couldn't swim freely through the water, could they?

Then, I saw a net, twisting with the current. It was empty.

I jumped from my seat, clambering over the dash to press my face against the glass. And, that's when I saw him: the half-incinerated body of my father, lying on a jagged bed of coral.

I screamed and cried and kicked my surroundings. I killed papa! He told me not to touch anything but I did! He was right; I was a fool! I killed papa! My stupidity, my clumsiness, my nothingness killed papa! I threw myself down on the floor. His words rang through my mind: 'I'd impale myself on a reef before letting my company pass to your hands!' Well, he was right!

I was tried as a juvenile for accidental manslaughter, so I didn't face much punishment besides that inflicted by my own anguished conscious. Ages passed and I strove to change everything about myself and become the man my father would've loved. Every day, I studied and exercised, until I was eighteen and allowed to enlist in the Diving Fleet as a voluntary adult. After a couple nightmarish ages as a surface-rider, I gladly returned home and answered my true calling: the business world. I became the engineer of the first stern-ramp and double-boom fishing vessel.

Along the way, I married a co-worker, Qui Tsop, and the two of us tried unceasingly to start a family. After seven miscarriages, our first and only child was finally born at Krustallos Finire Hospital in Nox City on the winter solstice of the seventy-fifth age—the twenty-eighth anniversary of my father's death. We named our son Cease Terminus Lechatelierite, after the great sea captain.

Cease was tiny—four pounds, seven ounces—but there was nothing small about his voice. He came into the world with eyes wide open, like two beacons of silver-grey light, screaming louder than I thought possible, considering how little his throat was. Intelligence already seemed to leap forth from the brilliant clarity of his stare. His skin was a translucent, glacier-white and he had dense patches of thick, dark fur on his head.

There were a few unwanted guests in attendance on Cease's birthday. Military personnel.

"No!" Qui cried before any of them spoke a word. "Cease is MY son! He's MINE!" She hugged him protectively.

"Please leave," I said to them.

Cease, no longer crying, looked up at all of us with those astute eyes, turning his head back and forth as though he were actually following.

A young officer named Autoero Austere wordlessly furnished the enlistment forms I signed, so many ages ago. According to the contract, the military had more rights to my son's life than me.

The ages that followed were cold and empty. I threw myself all the more into my work, using it to cope with Cease's loss. It was a decade before we heard another word from the Trilateral Committee. At age ten, they said, Cease graduated into the fleet. He was the officer of unit seven.

I figured, if Cease had to be locked into the military world, he might as well become the tycoon of it, as I was of the business world. As Cease's name quickly became legend, I felt something my father never had the chance to experience himself: pride in my son's achievements.

By then, my business had expanded far beyond commercial fishing. We were the pinnacle of warship manufacturing. January of this age, Qui and I traversed the sea to relocate to Alcove City, the most progressive place on Second Earth. A few months later, in August, our son declared victory in the sixteen-age war against the South Conflagrablaze Captive. Success was synonymous with the name Lechatelierite and I was never happier.

Qui and I were a nervous wreck the late-August day we were allowed to visit Cease for the first time. Icicle sent a small plane to pick us up, piloted by a tall, lanky, tan-skinned, blonde-haired, hazel-eyed diver who looked about nineteen.

"Mr. and Mrs. Lechatelierite, it's an honor," he breathed, taking each of our hands in turn, eyes alight. "I'm Unit Two Officer Nurtic Leavesleft and I'll be your cabbie for the day. The Admiral doesn't know you're coming, but I think he'll be pleasantly surprised."

"Cease doesn't know we're coming?" Qui echoed, twisting a lock of hair around her index finger.

"Don't worry," Leavesleft said as we took off. "He'll be glad to see you."

"Are you sure about that?" I asked, thinking about the base-raised divers I served alongside during my brief stint at Icicle. They were cold and calloused. They regarded relationship as a threat to their militancy and could hardly hold non-work-related conversations. My father was no exception. It was a wonder he was able to marry, once retired. My mother was a saint, to stand him all those ages.

A sudden visit from long-lost parents would be hard on anyone, let alone a base-raised soldier who'd been taught since birth that love and attachment were bad and forbidden. At least, if Cease were warned in advance, he could try to prepare a little. He could consult a counselor or, at least, his Nurian comrades. But, instead, he was about to be blindsided. This wasn't a surprise I wanted to spring on him. I wasn't about to ambush a military genius.

"Yes, I'm sure." A dimpled smile snuck across Leavesleft's face. "I wouldn't say so, a couple months ago, but he's changed a lot over the summer. You'll be okay." And, he laughed. This man was so animated, so full of life.

"Let me guess; you're Nurian?" I asked.

He nodded. "From your city."

My city. I supposed he meant Alcove City. I still thought of Nox, Ichthyosis as 'my city.'

"How long have you been serving?" The cobalt-blue sea sped beneath our wings.

"I started at the Nurian Diving Academy in October and graduated into the fleet in May."

And, the war ended in July. This boy was greener than green.

"Why would Cease be alright with seeing us now, but not back in the spring?" Qui asked delicately.

There was a long pause. I figured Leavesleft probably didn't know.

"He's been in the fleet for three months," I whispered to Qui. "I imagine he'd have to know Cease pretty well, to answer that."

"But, I do," said Leavesleft, who apparently had the ears of a hawk. "To an extent, anyway. But, I was much closer to his Second—we were friends."

"Friends?" Qui sqeaked. "But, the Laws of Emotional Protection…"

"Are impossible to enforce consistently," Leavesleft finished her sentence. "For the most part, the base-raised tend to obey, but more so because they actually believe in the theory behind the laws, not because they fear punishment. We Nurians break them all the time, though—most of us are friends and maybe half of us have illegal sentimental trinkets, hidden away somewhere. As long as you're discreet about it, chances are, you're not going to get court-martialed for talking to your comrades about personal stuff or keeping a photo of your family or girlfriend in your locker."

That much was true. During my service, most of us adult-recruits found ways to have furtive friendships and several of us kept knick-knacks stowed away. We just didn't do anything out in the open.

"Punishments only tend to be dished out for the bigger, more blatant violations," Leavesleft went on. "Like, if someone has a romantic relationship or does something sexual. Stuff like that. And, even that's really hard to prove. You'd need a witness or a confession or something. A guy did get iced last month, but only because I quite literally forced him to fess up."

"What did he do?" Qui asked.

"He tried to rape my friend," he said, darkly.

When I lived at Icicle, there were maybe three or four females around, all older ladies who worked in the kitchen or hospital. Did this man attack a middle-aged woman on the maintenance or medical crew? Or, perhaps, another male comrade?

"Anyway, the Admiral and I aren't the best of friends, but we have a solid professional relationship," Leavesleft continued. He sure was chatty. "I'm the officer of unit two, so I've been working with him fairly closely."

A Nurian, fresh out of the academy, already had such a high rank? How did Leavesleft manage that? He must've really impressed my son. And, my son must've really trusted him. Which brought us back to…

"So, you would know why Cease changed?" I pressed. Did Cease unwind because of his victory? No, that couldn't be it; my dad won a war, too, and he stayed on-edge until his dying day.

Leavesleft's cheeks adopted a slight pink twinge. "Yes, sir."

"And?"

He blinked. "I-I'm sorry, but I can't tell you."

"Why? Is it classified?"

"Well, no."

"Then, what's the problem?"

He drummed his fingers on the dash. "I'm actually not supposed to know. I found out by accident."

"What?"

"And, it's not just you; I can't tell anyone. Not as long as the Admiral is active-duty. It could end his career or be used for blackmail. Everyone in the fleet is undyingly devoted to him—I know I am—but, that doesn't mean it's safe to spill. Most importantly, it can never reach the Trilateral Committee."

Now, my curiosity was escalating to agonized suspense. Was my son a war criminal?

"Sir, I understand if you want to protect him," I said. "But, we're his parents. You don't need to protect him from us. We didn't raise Cease, but we still love him. We wouldn't dare leak something that could hurt him. We'd guard his secret fiercely."

Leavesleft was silent.

I exhaled through tight lips. It took all the discipline I had not to sock this Nurian in his dimpled face. But, in my fifties, I knew better than to try attacking a young, in-practice diving officer, even one who seemed so mellow and gentle. It'd likely be the last thing I ever did.

"Sir," Qui pleaded, "we haven't seen our son since the day he was born. We spent the last seventeen ages wondering about him, desperately. Please, you can trust us. Like my husband said, we wouldn't dream of distributing information that could be used against him."

Leavesleft scrunched his sandy brows together. What on Second Earth did Cease do? What was so terrible, this boy couldn't tell the two people in the world who cared most for his wellbeing?

Leavesleft must've noticed the worry on my face, because then he said, "Mr. Lechatelierite, don't be alarmed. He didn't do anything bad."

"Well, it clearly *is* bad, if word of it could destroy him," I retorted.

"It's illegal…but not bad. He'll probably even tell you himself. I'll let him make that call. It's his secret to share, not mine."

Illegal, but not bad. Not bad in the eyes of a green, nineteen-age-old Nurian.

"He broke the Laws of Emotional Protection," I said, "and not just to make a friend. He broke them in a big way, a way that'd get him court-martialed, if the Trilateral Committee got wind of it. Am I right?"

Fear struck Leavesleft's entire figure. That gave me my answer.

Qui giggled like a schoolgirl. "Who's the lucky gal? I didn't know there are women at Icicle."

My chest tightened. If Cease fell for a forty-age-old, cafeteria cook, I was going to kill him.

"There are a few," Leavesleft answered, "mostly maintenance and medical staff. But, one was your son's second-in-command. The only female diver in Ichthyothian military history. We were good friends. I met her over an age ago, back in Alcove City, before we enlisted. She's a remarkable person."

And, apparently, Nurian. So, Cease's illegal romance was with a soldier of lofty rank and similar age. What a relief. I wasn't thrilled she was Nurian—I knew I'd need some time to warm up to the idea. But, things could've been way worse. I exhaled.

Qui laughed, tossing back her hair. "Only one girl and Cease snagged her. Atta boy."

"You can't tell anyone," Leavesleft said. "This could wreck his life. I'm serious. Promise you won't say anything, to anyone."

"We promise, we promise!" Qui chuckled, gleefully.

"So, this relationship could be out in the open, once they're retired?" I asked.

Leavesleft chewed his lip. "Well, technically, I guess."

"Has Cease mentioned anything about retirement plans?"

"No. I, um, don't think he'd want to go."

Married to the job, just like his old man. He clearly loved his work more than he loved whoever she was.

Qui deflated. "Why not? The war's over and Cease has an incentive to retire. I'd love it if he came home, and with a girlfriend!"

"Well…she…isn't really around, anymore."

"She *died?*" Qui screeched.

"No, no, she went home, a couple weeks ago. And, she, um, doesn't intend to come back."

She retired and left him?

"They broke up?" Qui breathed. "Poor Cease!"

"She left Icicle only because she had to. Her hand was forced by outside circumstances. She has important things to tend to, back home."

I cleared my throat. "Back home in Alcove City?"

Joystick clutched tightly in Leavesleft's left hand, his right fluttered to the little cross around his neck.

"Is she from Alcove City?" I insisted.

"That's where we first met," he said, blinking a little too often, "before the academy."

"In high school?"

"N-no."

"Then, where?" Alcove City was enormous.

"The train station."

"In transit?" Why was Leavesleft making us pull this from him like teeth?

"No, not exactly. I was there for the arcade and she was…"

"Yes?" I pressed.

"Um…at work. She worked there, as a conductor."

What? "How old is she, exactly?"

"Sixteen."

A teenage train conductor?

"Sixteen!" Qui exclaimed. "She's a child!"

"Well, the Admiral's only seventeen, so…" Leavesleft said.

I touched my moustache. "So, she's back in Alcove City now, tending to personal matters. Family matters?"

Silence.

"Sir?" I pressed.

"Well, she, um…doesn't have a family. I'm not entirely sure why."

"An orphan!" Qui cooed. "Oh, poor baby!"

"*No* family, at all?"

Leavesleft shook his head.

"Then, what did she need to go back home for?" Qui asked. "And, who's she staying with?"

"She said she kind of always…took care of herself."

"What do you mean, 'took care of herself'?" I demanded. "She's a minor. Are you telling me, before she enlisted, she was some sort of street beggar?"

Leavesleft winced. "She's a brave, resourceful woman who fought against all odds to make a life for herself. And, she changed the course of history, while she was at it."

I glared. "You're telling me Cease fell for some Nurian vagabond—"

"She's the most brilliant person I ever met, aside from your son," Leavesleft cut across me. "I don't know what would've become of the alliance, if she never served."

"She left Icicle to go back to the city streets?" Qui peeped. "That doesn't make any sense."

Leavesleft looked as though he were about to explode. "She…didn't go back to Nuria."

I rounded on him. "Quit playing games and tell us straight: did she or did she not leave Icicle?"

Leavesleft swallowed. "She did, sir. But, not for Nuria." He inhaled. "She went home…to fight in the Conflagrian Civil War."

Qui went pale. "She's…Conflagrian? One of those… savage, magic-people?"

I felt my body temperature rise. "How could a Conflagrian join the Nurro-Ichthyothian Military, in the first place?"

"She passed as Nurian. I didn't know the truth until the very end of July, right before she left, none of us did. Except Lechatelierite. He knew she was a mage from the start, but didn't tell anyone. He determined she had pure motives and could be trusted, so he allowed her to stay. She was like his secret weapon or something."

"She bewitched him!" Qui roared. "She manipulated his heart so he'd promote her to where she'd have access to all the big, military secrets! And, now, she's run off to share everything with the enemy!"

"No," Leavesleft objected, "no, you've got it all wrong. She's with the Red Revolution, now. They're the good guys. The System is the alliance's only enemy. I've trusted Scarlet July with my life—everyone in the fleet has—and she never let us down. She's the reason we won the war."

I snorted. "My son won the war! I've never even heard the name 'Scarlet July' before, and you're telling me she's the one behind the Crystal's end?"

Leavesleft tore his gaze from the windshield again, hazel eyes solemn as they bored into me. "Yes, sir," he said, voice uncharacteristically hard, "I do expect you to believe the third-ranking officer of the Diving Fleet when he tells you how the war ended. I actually participated in the Conflagrian infiltration and directly assisted Scarlet July and the Admiral in destroying the Core Crystal. My word should carry more weight to you than anything the media says—or doesn't say."

I looked away, confused and embarrassed and infuriated, all at once.

"And, I'd also expect you to put a little more faith in your son's judgment,' Leavesleft continued. "The Leader of the Nurro-Ichthyothian Resistance isn't gullible or stupid and has the right to trust, promote and love whoever he sees fit. Scarlet July is a good choice. A great choice. She's a heroine who put everything on the line for the alliance."

I chortled. "I see she has you under her spell, too. Mages are malicious and cunning. And, no matter his credentials or military prowess, Cease is still a hormonal teenager who's never seen an age-appropriate girl in his life before this mage came along. So, no, I don't trust his judgment when it comes to this. Especially if a Conflagrian is involved."

Leavesleft's knuckles went pale on the joystick. The three of us rode in silence the rest of the way.

At last, we landed. Qui and I followed Leavesleft into the snow. My eyes drank in the wintery beauty, all around us. Frost collected on my moustache as my breath curled into the air. The air smelled clean and crisp, compared to the polluted stench of Alcove City. It was wonderful to be home.

Apparently, Leavesleft didn't share my sentiment. He cast a displeased eye at the overcast sky as he led the way. Qui's face was as white as a glacier. She squeezed my hand as we went inside and met a diver with an expressionless, woodchip-pale stare. Base-raised Ichthyothian, no doubt.

"Frappe," Leavesleft greeted the man with a smile he didn't return. "Could you please inform the Admiral he has guests?"

Frappe nodded and turned on his heel.

Five minutes—which felt more like five eras—passed before Frappe returned with my son. My heart pounded against my ribcage as they approached from the end of a long, narrow corridor. Cease looked so small and slight next to his comrade. I wondered if he inherited his grand-father's mild proportionate-dwarfism. It certainly skipped my generation.

From beside me, Qui sniffed and dabbed her eyes with a red handkerchief.

It was hard to tell from afar, but something was obstructing Cease's face. I only recognized what it was when he turned his head and it caught the florescent light: a visual reparation band. I hadn't seen one of those in ages. What couldn't be fixed with laser surgery, these days? Was my grandfather's sight issue an inheritable birth defect? I always assumed it was a battle-scar.

Soon, they were close enough for their conversation to be audible.

"Your guests won't be able to stay long, as they have business matters to tend to, back home," Frappe told Cease. "And, the Trilateral Committee thought it best to keep things brief."

"What are you talking ab—" Cease stopped dead when he caught sight of us. He slowly pulled his band off.

"Mother?" he whispered. "Father?"

"We're proud of you, son," I said.

Qui ran to him. "Oh, Cease, we didn't want to give you up, we really didn't," she sobbed into his ear. "But, we had no choice!"

For a moment, Cease just stood there like a statue and let her hug him, face deadpan. It was a while before he thought to put his arms around her, too. He did so awkwardly, elbows out.

"Don't worry," he said, solemnly. "No other parents will have to go through what you've been through, handing over their newborns to the military. I'll see to that myself. I promise."

Those words were like a breath of fresh, Ichthyothian winter air on a sticky, Nurian summer day. I knew his promise could never restore his childhood or erase what my father put my mother and I through because of what the Childhood Program put *him* through. But, it was the next best thing. And, I figured, if a war hero swore to do something, it was as good as done.

Our eyes locked for a moment in silent understanding.

I heard movement to my left. I turned and saw Leavesleft a few feet away, dimples twitching, looking at his boots. He probably felt like an intruder on our family reunion.

Cease's colorless gaze followed mine. "Dismissed, Leavesleft," he ordered coldly, giving a rather scathing look to the very subordinate who said he'd die for him. If this was Cease as a changed man, I didn't want to know what he was like before the summer.

Leavesleft didn't leave. "Sir, I'm supposed to escort all of you to a designated conference room." He turned to Qui and I. "Mr. and Mrs. Lechatelierite, you have thirty minutes before your return-flight to Alcove City."

"Thirty minutes?" Qui piped.

"What's the meaning of this?" I raged.

"I'm sorry, sir, ma'am." And, he did indeed look very sorry. "This is by order of the Trilateral Committee."

"We've had enough of the Trilateral Committee!" Qui cried. "They've already deprived us of our child, his whole life! They've had plenty of him!"

"I don't understand their strictness, considering the war's over," I growled.

Poor Leavesleft absorbed our anger. "I'm sorry, I really am. But, please, let's not waste the time you do have. Follow me to the designated room. Right this way."

"This is outrageous!" Qui wrung her handkerchief.

Cease didn't make a sound, angular face set. If he was bothered by the time limit, he didn't show it. He just walked with us, hands clasped behind his back, staring off, as if heading to just another mundane, officers' meeting.

Already, I couldn't imagine him conducting a romantic relationship. For a brief moment, I actually felt bad for Scarlet July, as I always did for my mother.

We entered the 'designated room.' Leavesleft looked relieved as he bid us farewell and closed the door behind him.

Silence.

"Sit down," Cease ordered stiffly.

We sat.

Qui blew her nose loudly. Cease regarded her. I watched as his stern eyes studied her face and posture, as though she were a new subordinate for him to analyze and use. I recognized the caliber of that calculating look because I'd received it countless times from my father, growing up.

Qui leaned forward and took Cease's hands in hers. He visibly flinched.

"Speak to us, son," she said, breathless. "Tell us something, anything. We've waited seventeen ages to see your face and hear your voice."

Cease blinked. Good; I was starting to wonder if he ever broke his stare long enough to close his lids. But, he still didn't speak.

I remembered how much it meant to me when my father clapped my shoulder for the first and only time. So, I went ahead and touched Cease's slight, bony shoulder. But, apparently, he didn't understand the gesture; he yanked his hands from Qui's and caught my wrist, tightly. His eyes raked my face, frosty enough to freeze fire. I fought the urge to look away.

Did he think I was attacking him or what? Why would I?

I made myself chortle. "Good reflexes; I see they've trained you well!"

Qui gave me an exasperated glance that seemed to say: sure, if by 'trained well,' you mean 'inflicted with severe paranoia.'

"Thank you," Cease said monotonously, letting go. The sensation rushed back to my fingertips.

Qui actually had the courage reach for his hand again—just one, this time—and give his hardened face a sweet smile.

"So, how do you feel, Cease? After sixteen ages, the war's over; you led your nation to victory!"

Cease blinked, again. "It's quite a relief."

Quite a relief? "Is that all?" I asked, forcing myself to smile like Qui. My son was an emotional sinkhole. "You fulfilled your life's purpose; surely, that's more than just a relief!"

"My life's purpose," he echoed. "At seventeen, I fulfilled my life's purpose. So, my existence is pointless, now?"

"Oh, no, no," Qui responded, quickly. "What your father meant by that is—"

"What if war isn't my only purpose?" he shot. "What if I'm capable of something other than killing? Have you considered that?"

This was going downhill fast. But, I didn't drop my cheery demeanor, determined to smooth things over. "Well, clearly, you are where you're meant to be, son; just look at all you've done!"

Couldn't he see how proud we were? Growing up, I would've killed for my father to say those words to me. I would've killed to make it through the Childhood Program instead of living out my youth in the shadow of my failure.

Cease's eyes were molten iron. A strange, acherontic air seemed to hover around him. What was that eerie, black haze?

"So, that's all there is to me?" he spat. "I am what I've done in the war?"

"Of course not," Qui said.

What was wrong with Cease? Back when I served, soldiers were respectful and disciplined. Why was Cease jumping all over us and going out of his way to misinterpret my praise? Was it because he resented us for turning him over to the military?

Apparently, Qui was thinking the same thing. "Please remember," she stroked the back of his hand, "Finis and I didn't *want* to give you up. We weren't the ones who determined your career path. Officers came to Krustallos Finire Hospital the day you were born and took you from our arms. It's the worst thing that's ever happened to us."

For a second, my son's face changed; his shell cracked and he regarded her with warmth and concern. Was this what Leavesleft was talking about? Was this a glimpse into the new Cease?

Almost as soon as the sympathetic look came, it went.

"Finis?" His gaze shifted to me. "That's your name?"

He didn't know our names? Did he even know we were alive, until today? Did he ever think of us? Did he realize how abnormal his upbringing was? He must have, to some extent, because he promised to dismantle the Childhood Program.

"Yes. Finis Arrete."

Cease turned to Qui. "And, you?"

Qui swallowed. "Qui. And, Tsop was my maiden name, so now I've made it my middle name."

"Finis Arrete and Qui Tsop Lechatelierite," he repeated. "What are your jobs? Where do you live? Frappe said something about a business in Nuria?"

We were talking to a total stranger.

"I'm the CEO of the Nurro-Ichthyothian Underwater Vessel Manufacturing Company, and your mother is our top technical writer," I answered proudly.

Cease seemed about as moved by his long-lost parents' wild success as he was by the fact he ended an international war just weeks prior. Did anything make him smile?

"How long have you been living in Nuria?"

"Since January. We're based out of the Nurian Trade Centerscraper in Alcove City. Before that, we lived in Nox, a nocturnatown in central Ichthyosis, where you were born."

"Were you a part of Nox's day or night population?"

"Night. We petitioned to switch to day-shift every age since seventy-five, but never got in. I'm glad Nuria has no such system: actually sleeping when it's dark and waking when it's light is just about the only thing your mother and I like about living in Alcove City."

There came a knock at the door. When it opened, there stood a young soldier with puffy, curly, brown hair. Curly hair was really uncommon, both in Nuria and Ichthyosis. If I didn't know better, I'd guess this man were Orion.

Cease squinted at him then resigned to strapping on his visual band. Just how blind was he?

"Yes, Link?"

"I'm sorry for the intrusion, Admiral," Link piped in Nurian. "Just reminding you of your video-conference with Commander Slue and Commander Zephyr at thirty-one o' clock."

"I don't need a reminder, but tell the Trilateral Committee thanks for using you to interrupt my time with my parents," Cease retorted in Nurian. His Ichthyothian accent was very thick. "Dismissed."

Link scurried away.

Cease looked at us through his reflective band. "That was Arrhyth Link, the sub-leader of unit eleven."

I wondered if curly-haired Arrhyth Link was related to Arnold Link, the Orion Chairman of the Second Earth Order. That'd be crazy. But, as curious as I was, I wasn't about to spend any of my precious time with Cease asking about it.

Cease pulled his band back off and began shoving it under his collar, but Qui reached out and took it right from his hands. My wife was a brave woman.

"What happened to your eyes, Cease?" She surveyed the tiny mechanisms on the inside of the arc. "Why do you need this thing?"

His face tightened. So, we hit a sensitive topic.

"Why not just get laser surgery, if you're nearsighted or something?" Qui asked, still perusing the contraption.

Cease pursed his thin lips. "Laser surgery has helped, but the severity of my injury necessitates the use of a visual reparation band for sight maintenance."

"What?"

"I could go blind without it."

Injury. So, Cease's vision issues weren't genetic; he had a lasting battle scar. That's why the topic was sensitive—his pride was wounded along with his sight.

"Injury!" She wrung the arc in her hands. "What happened?"

Cease snatched it from her and hastily tucked it away. "I was surface-riding thousands of feet deep when my suit got scorched by the System's Underwater Fire, subjecting my head and body to extreme water pressure. I also had a concussion, from shuttle debris."

"Oh no!" Qui survyed Cease, up and down. "Are you okay?" She squeezed his hand as though to protect him from his past.

"I am, now."

"Now?"

"I was…paralyzed, for a while."

Paralyzed!? A gear jammed in my mind. My son—my strong, brilliant, successful son—was once a *cripple?*

"When was this?" Qui asked.

"An age ago."

"Only?"

"Yes," Cease said, testily.

"You're totally recovered now, aside from the eye thing?"

"Yes!"

"You recovered from *paralysis* in only an age?"

"I've been well enough for combat since the start of summer."

It was still summer, now. "You mean since a month or two ago?" I interjected.

"Just long enough to win the war," Cease shot.

"Oh, poor baby!" Qui wailed.

"This is war." Cease voice was loud and mad. "I don't know why you two are so shocked at the idea of a *soldier* getting injured in a *war*."

"That was the battle you lost," I suddenly spouted, "wasn't it?"

Cease glared at me. But, I no longer saw light in those silver eyes. All I could see was damage and defect. He didn't answer. Which gave me the answer.

"How did you make it out alive?" Qui asked, literally at the edge of her seat.

A slight, sad smile tugged the corners of Cease's lips. It was the first smile I saw from him, yet. "Forget scorched, I would've burned alive with the crystalline if weren't for Scarlet."

I sat up straight as a lance. "If that battle was an age ago, it was before the alliance!" I half-shouted. "Scarlet July couldn't have possibly been there!"

Cease stared at me, shocked. "How do you know Scarlet came from Nuria? The Trilateral Committee kept her completely out of the media. How do you even know her name?"

I was seeing red, disappointment in Cease mounting. "I know she's a fire-savage who begged on the city streets before lying and manipulating her way into your life!"

In a flash, Cease sprung up, seized my collar and bodily slammed me into the wall behind us, knocking over my chair in the process—never mind our significant physical discrepancy. His diamond stare pierced my face as he breathed loudly through his nostrils. His inexplicable, freaky black glow darkened and thickened.

Qui screamed, "Cease, let go of him! How dare you get violent with your father!"

Cease, still glaring, released me. And, the instant he did, I struck his bony cheek with the back of my hand. Qui gasped.

"You owe me some respect, boy!" I barked.

"For what? DNA hardly makes you a father. You didn't raise me, you don't even know me! Scarlet July *earned* my respect. But, you immediately write me off as some heartless robot whose only purpose in life is to kill!"

There was a quick knock at the door, followed by the creak of it opening.

"Excuse me, sirs, ma'am, this is your three-minute warning—" Leavesleft stopped dead when he caught sight of our angry faces and my overturned chair. "I-I'm sorry for interrupting. I was just—"

"Leavesleft," Cease cut him off, "get the hell out of here!"

"Yes, sir!" He fled the scene.

Silence.

I watched as Cease slowly picked up my chair, setting it on its legs.

"Sit," he ordered.

I sat.

Qui folded her red handkerchief on her lap and the faint rustle seemed to fill the whole room.

"Cease," she squawked, "Finis and I need to tell you something. Something we've wanted to tell you for seventeen ages." She swallowed. "We love you, son. No matter what. And, if we got to raise you, we would've been sure to tell you that, every day."

Cease didn't move or blink. He didn't say he loved us, too. He didn't even say, thank you. He just sat there, eyes vacant.

The door squeaked. Leavesleft was back. Time to go. He waited in the hall for us to say our last good-byes.

We stood. Qui threw her arms around Cease again. He didn't even attempt to hug her back, this time. When she let go, I touched his arm and felt his muscles tighten beneath my fingertips. I actually would've liked to embrace him too, but his body language made it abundantly clear it wouldn't be welcome.

Cease's silver-grey gaze hovered aimlessly in the air, between Qui and I. "I wish I could say I feel the same way," he said, voice barely audible. "It's not your fault I can't say those words back. But, remember my promise." His eyes met mine. "That's one thing I can give to you."

I nodded, throat tight. Qui started crying noisily.

And, with that, Cease walked right out the door, disappearing down the corridor without looking back.

FINIS LECHATELIERITE

January second. The first workday of the ninety-fourth age.

At seven o'clock, I had an appointment with the leader of the Conflagrian rebellion. I never heard much about the so-called 'Red Revolution.' It wasn't like Conflagria communicated much with the outside world. They didn't have the means to do so without difficulty, nor was the alliance particularly interested in getting involved in their civil war. Conflagrians could kill each other all they wanted; we only cared if they wreaked havoc outside their own boarders.

Frankly, I wasn't really sure what to expect from today's meeting; I only agreed to it because I figured this 'Red Leader,' whoever he was, would be able to shed some light on how exactly the System was managing to pillage our ports.

"Mr. Lechatelierite," came the voice of my secretary on the intercom, "the Conflagrian Revolutionary Leader has arrived."

"I requested a translator," I reminded her. It was quite an expensive ordeal, getting authorization for an interpreter, since the Second Earth Order was the only organization on the planet permitted to have any. "Send them both up."

"That won't be necessary, sir. Your guest claims to be fluent in Ichthyothian, Nurian and Conflagrian."

Wow. Who besides Order staff and Nurro-Ichthyothian military personnel would bother learning multiple languages and how? I guessed I'd send the translator straight back to Oriya. What a waste of paperwork and money.

"Very well, then. He may enter."

A minute later, the door creaked open, and in came a very young, short, scrawny, red-faced, red-haired, green-eyed girl in a blood-red robe overtop a brown vest and a pleated, nearly-knee-length, brown skirt.

"Hello, Mr. Lechatelierite, sir. I am the Leader of the Conflagrian Red Revolution, Scarlet July," she said in perfect Ichthyothian, without a trace of an accent. "Pleased to meet you." She held out a rather frail-looking hand.

I stared. It was *her*. I pressed my lips together. After a long, uncomfortable pause, I briefly took her hot, bony hand in mine, suppressing a shudder.

"Thank you," I said stiffly, too dumbfounded to introduce myself or say I was also pleased to meet her. I gestured to the chair across from my desk. She hopped into it, feet unable to reach the floor while seated. I looked distastefully at the frayed hem of her tattered robe and her dirty, worn-out sandals, laced halfway up her calves. She was getting grime and dust all over my nice, black leather. She couldn't clean herself up a bit before meeting with the CEO of the finest industry on the coast? "What brings you here, Miss July?"

"Sir, my co-leader, Ambrek Coppertus, recently discovered the presence of a fragment of the Core Crystal at the bottom of the Briny Ocean," she launched directly into business, militant demeanor clashing with her childlike appearance. "It's still active, so it could potentially restore the spectral web—and, along with it, the mind-control of the System." I noticed that she, like my son, tended to stare without blinking. "We need to retrieve and destroy this fragment before the System finds it. If they get to it first, they will deposit it into the Fire Pit, where it would take root and develop. And, as it grows, the web will crystallize, reversing the diffusion that occurred in July. Everything the Nurro-Ichthyothian Diving Fleet accomplished last summer would be undone; the alliance would be back to square one."

The civilian world wasn't too familiar with the details of how the Diving Fleet 'won' the war, last summer. We knew it had something to do with a crystal, but anything beyond that wasn't public knowledge. Qui and I read every news story on the 'victory' we could find, but they all just seemed to use a lot of pretty words to relay next to nothing. I wasn't sure if the details were classified or if the journalists writing the articles didn't understand much, themselves. So, Scarlet's blurb now, filled with strange terms like 'crystallize' and 'diffusion,' made little sense to me.

"Finding the shard would require an underwater craft, which the Reds don't have," she went on, never taking her large, glassy eyes off my face. "I came here today to ask if your company would be willing to loan us a couple scuba suits and a single submarine, equipped with minimal weapons, if possible."

She was so strange. Her delicate features and high cheekbones would've made her conventionally attractive if it weren't for the red blotchiness of her skin and the uncanny enormity of her eyes. Her eccentricity overwhelmed what beauty she might've had.

Scarlet finally blinked. "Would that be possible, Mr. Lechatelierite, sir?"

Her emerald eyes were so astute, so alert, they would've been intimidating, if they weren't peering from the thin face of a little girl. She was a warrior? How laughable. How did her fellow 'revolutionaries' take her seriously? How did the men in my son's fleet follow her into combat?

What did Cease see in her?

I cleared my throat. "According to the Second War Pact of the Ninety-Second Age, only Nurians and Ichthyothians are permitted to join the Nurro-Ichthyothian military, correct?"

Scarlet looked confused. For a soldier, her face sure was readable. "Yes, sir, that's true."

"So, you knew you were breaking the law when you joined the Diving Fleet?"

"S-sir," she sputtered like a kid in the principal's office, "could we please stay on topic—"

"Because *you* broke the law, *my son* is in jail!"

Her eyes went wide, dominating her face all the more. "Jail?" she gasped, sitting up straighter. "Cease is in jail?"

"Don't pull that doe-eyed act on me," I growled, "pretending that isn't why you ran off right after the war 'ended,' leaving my son alone to face court-martial!"

"Court-martial?" she cried, trembling. She was either genuinely surprised or a fantastic actress. "Sir, how could I've known?"

"See for yourself!" I tossed a copy of the *Alcove City Post* at her. "He lost his career *and* his mind, over *you!*"

Scarlet's eyes tore down the page. "PTSD? Hallucinations?" She breathed, apparently more alarmed by his mental deterioration than the total demolition of his career. She looked up at me. "Sir, he isn't hallucinating, he's having visions! It says here, he saw the Red Leader take a torch to the head during a sandstorm, and that he's afraid there's something in the sea bringing Conflagria's spectrum back. He's right! He's telling the truth! No wonder he's having 'violent outbursts'—his warnings are being ignored!" A tear snuck down her pink cheek. "Oh, poor Cease, I believe you, Cease, I believe you!"

"Enough!" I growled. "Nordics can't have visions! He's gone mad, hallucinating about you and your hocus pocus magic tricks!"

"He hasn't gone mad!" Scarlet yelled, voice high-pitched. "He needs to be taken seriously!"

"This meeting's over!" I snatched the paper from Scarlet's hands. "No, you may not have a ship! Get out of my office!"

"You have to believe him, sir!" Scarlet reached across the desk and grabbed my shoulders. "Cease is having visions—"

"SECURITY!"

The door banged open and two guards burst in.

"Remove this Conflagrian from my building! And, see to it she doesn't lay a hand on any of my ships!"

"Yes, sir."

The guards yanked Scarlet's wiry arms behind her back and ushered her out the door. Now, she got a little taste of what my son endured when marched out of Icicle in cuffs.

FAIR GABARDINE

I sat on the curb across the street from the Nurian Trade Centerscraper, an impossibly tall building checkered with shiny, tinted windows, like dragon scales. The CEO of the Nurro-Ichthyothian Underwater Vessel Manufacturing Company agreed to meet with Scarlet, as she was the 'Revolutionary Leader.' I, however, was denied entrance, my presence deemed 'unnecessary.'

I sighed and watched as heavily-polluting flivvers chugged through the crowded streets. The cloudy, blue-grey sky hung overhead. The air was stale, smelly and cold, all at once. Compared to the brilliant, red-orange sunshine of Conflagria, the capital of Nuria was dark and dingy. The architecture was a strange mix of off-white concrete, bluish glass and silver-grey metal. Police flivver-chases were commonplace; passerby gave but mere, disinterested glances. Last night, Scarlet and I slept behind the train station, where she used to work. I couldn't believe that dirty, trash-cluttered alley was her home for five ages. And, Nordics thought Conflagria was the 'third world'? I didn't see how dumpy Alcove City was any more 'civilized' than Ardor Village.

I glanced at the large, digital timepiece fixed over the main entrance of the Centerscraper and saw that Scarlet had been inside for only fifteen minutes now, though it felt more like fifteen eras. There seemed to be clocks on every corner, around here. Apparently, Nurians felt the need to monitor every second of their day. Never mind that their days were already ridiculously long to begin with—even after five months, I was yet to fully adapt to a thirty-six-hour cycle.

Along with clocks, there were also lots of giant screens everywhere, playing advertisements and news broadcasts. I didn't understand Nurian, but I watched anyway, because it was either that or count flivvers.

My jaw unhinged when the TVs displayed Cease Lechatelierite being ushered into a police plane in cuffs, looking even thinner and more feral than I remembered him. Why in the world would Ichthyosis arrest their top military leader? Was he finally getting what he deserved for shooting the Geneva Convention to hell? I wished I could understand what the news anchor was saying. Scarlet was going to go berserk when she saw this. *If* she saw this. It'd be better if we flew away the second she got out, so she'd be spared the heartache of seeing her beloved Cease in chains and I'd be spared her inevitable, endless, lovesick, worried whining.

Thirty minutes and counting. I sat in nervous anticipation, wondering and waiting. I had confidence in Scarlet's powers of persuasion and couldn't wait for her to emerge with a smile on her lips and the keys to a sub in her hands. If anyone knew how to get what they wanted, it was Scarlet. If she could worm her way up to second-in-command of the elite Nurro-Ichthyothian Diving Fleet after only eight months and make the Commander fall for her in two, she could certainly haggle a ship from some coffee-addicted, harried, Nurian businessman. It's not like she was going up against a military mind.

At last, from across the wide, multi-lane street, I saw Scarlet's tiny red figure appear…flanked by two angry-looking men with badges. Scarlet's hands were behind her back.

Uh oh.

I dove across the street, to the sound of flivvers screeching and honking.

"You didn't get the ship, did you?" I asked her in Conflagrian, the moment I reached the sidewalk.

She closed her wet eyes and shook her head. One of the guards bellowed at her in Nurian, then they released her and stalked back inside.

"What happened? Why didn't they give it to you?"

"He," she choked. "I met with just one man, the CEO. Cease's father."

My lips parted.

"Now, you see the problem?" she breathed.

I blinked. No, I didn't. So, what if the CEO was Cease's father? That shouldn't have made a difference. Scarlet was there to conduct business, not get personal. What in the world did they talk about? Why would Scarlet let their conversation stray when she knew what was at stake? Now, all we had left was Ambrek's ludicrous plan to kidnap System pilots and throw ourselves into a sea battle!

That was, if we ever got out of Nuria.

"Scarlet, how are we going to get home without a sub?"

We arrived on dragonback, yesterday evening. But, it wasn't in a pine dragon's nature to touch down on unfamiliar ground—at least, not until it got truly desperate for food or rest—so we had to jump off of it and swim a quarter-mile to shore. We hadn't counted on needing the beast, again. It could be anywhere, by now.

"Let's head for the ports," she croaked. "After a fifteen-hundred-mile flight, the dragon had to land, at some point." She hiccupped and began walking at a brisk pace.

I tailed her. "You mean, we're just going to wander around, looking for it?'"

"You and Ambrek seem totally convinced I'll be able to find a stone on the seafloor. If I can do that, I can track down a nine-hundred pound dragon stomping around the docks," she said acidly, wiping her face with her sleeve. "Pine dragons are afraid of the unknown; it can't have gone too far. Come on, let's go tell Ambrek we're ready for plan 'B.'"

SCARLET JULY

As Fair and I trudged through the streets of Alcove City, heading for the ports, I glanced at one of the massive, sky-scraper-side television screens and stopped dead at the sight of a suited man pointing at a map of Conflagria with a big bull's-eye over the northern region.

"…Yesterday evening's earthquake in northern Conflagria," the weatherman was saying, "caused a tsunami that swept through the Fervor Sea, Briny Ocean and Septentrion Sea, wiping out marine life and stirring up debris from the Ichthyo-Conflagrian War." My stomach jumped into my throat. Were Ambrek and those in Second, Third and Fourth Cabins alright? "Just to give you an idea of the power of this system," he went on, excitedly, "a fragment of the carrier that crashed into the Fervor Sea Base last July washed up on the shore of sector seven, Ichthyosis. That sector, which consists of about eighty square miles of seis-mically-unstable, uninhabited glacier-land, is…"

"What are they saying?" Fair's eyes raked my scandalized face. "Scarlet, what's going on?"

I translated for her and her cheeks turned a sick shade of yellow.

"But, if the current was strong enough to carry debris from the Fervor Sea all the way to Ichthyosis," she breathed, "wouldn't that also mean the crystal fragment…?"

"Probably. And, the Septentrion Sea is where the System and Ichthyosis have most of their naval battles." I swallowed. "Come on, Fair. We need to get home, right away." I started running. "We need to be there the next time the System deploys."

AMBREK COPPERTUS

Scarlet and Fair's absence made it easy for me to make the trek from Red Headquarters at the northern shore to the Mage Castle in Ardor Village, to meet with Principal Tiki Tincture and Captain Anapes Patrici. I didn't have to make up any lies or fake being kidnapped; I could just hop on a scabrous and go. I finally had my chance to break the big news to the System: Nuria and Ichthyosis were secret allies.

"A blockade," Anapes said, the moment the intel left my lips. "The Water Forces will initiate a blockade in the Septentrion Sea, starving out Ichthyosis."

"And, I will alert the Second Earth Order of the alliance's existence," the Principal said, "blacklisting Nuria."

Anapes folded his arms. "I can't believe, all this time, we've been at war with Nuria, too. Well, now that we have nothing to lose, I say we strike Nuria, directly. Raiding ports and blockading's only the beginning."

"What do you propose, sir?" I asked.

Anapes took a deep breath. "If Nurian industry is the reason Ichthyosis hasn't crumbled by now, I say we attack the pinnacle of Nordic wartime production. Let's bomb the Nurian Trade Centerscraper in Alcove City."

* * *

I returned to Headquarters late at night on the second, on scabrousback, startled to find the village in ruins. My jaw hung at the sight of countless uprooted trees and de-molished cabins. I was relieved our cabin was more or less intact—only a third of our roof was missing. What on earth happened, here?

Within minutes of my arrival, Fair and Scarlet also came home—talk about cutting it close. The second Scarlet walked through the door, she threw herself into my arms.

"I heard about the earthquake!" she cried. "Oh, thank Tincture you're alive! Are you alright?"

Earthquake? "I'm fine, I'm fine," I said, inhaling her wood-smoke scent. "It was terrible, but I made it through. You picked a good time to be away; I'm glad you were spared." As was I. Apparently, the quake didn't affect central or southern Conflagria.

"How're the others?" Fair asked. "Where's Prunus Persica; is he okay?"

I shrugged. "I don't know. Isn't he stationed at Seventh Cabin? I, um, don't think Ardor Village was hit. Too far south, I guess."

The Reds had seventeen strongholds in total, with ours known as 'First Cabin' or 'Headquarters.' Our strongholds were rather uncreatively named by Scarlet, 'First Cabin,' 'Second Cabin,' 'Third Cabin' and so forth. For Tincture's sake, Scarlet really did act like a stiff Ichthyothian, sometimes.

"Yeah, but we asked you to ask him to stay here while we're away, to help hold down the fort."

Right. They did tell me to do that. And, I totally forgot, caught up in my own plans.

"Prunus…couldn't make it," I said stupidly. "He was…busy."

Fair blinked. "Oh."

I needed to change the subject, right now. "So, shall we go outside and take a look at our new ship?" I grinned.

At this, Scarlet burst into tears like a child.

"Hey, hey, it's okay," I stroked Scarlet's wiry hair, alarmed. "It's not the end of the world if you didn't get it; we have a plan 'B.'"

But, Scarlet just sobbed harder. I gave Fair a quizzical look.

"It's about Cease," she said darkly, arms folded across her chest. At the mere mention of his name, confusion and jealousy prickled my chest. "Apparently, he's been suspended from duty and thrown in jail in Alcove City, awaiting court-martial for war crimes. It's all over the Nordic media."

"And, that's not all!" Scarlet cried into my robe. "Everyone thinks he's going crazy!"

I couldn't believe my ears. For the last couple ages, Lechatelierite's leadership was what kept the Ichthyothian Resistance alive. The Nordics were willingly holstering their most dangerous weapon? It was too good to be true.

"What are you smiling about?" Fair growled at me.

Shoot. "Uh, just thinking about how…absurd all this is." I resisted the urge to shove my foot in my mouth. "So, what happened at the meeting?"

Fair's oil-black eyes grew angry. "Don't ask me; I wasn't allowed in." She tossed her long hair over her shoulder. "Scarlet met with the CEO, himself. Cease's father."

What were the odds? "Cease's father is a Nurian business tycoon? Is Cease mixed or is the head of Nurian ship manufacturing an Ichthyothian?"

"He's Ichthyothian," Scarlet said.

"What difference does it make?" Fair snapped. "It shouldn't have mattered who he is or where he's from! This was supposed to be a business transaction! I don't know how their conversation derailed or why Mr. Lechatelierite felt the need to throw Scarlet out with security on her back!"

"I told you, I didn't provoke him!" Scarlet wrenched herself from my arms and wheeled around to face Fair. "I tried hard to stay on topic; he's the one who got all personal, accusing me of breaking his son's heart and driving him mad!"

What? "How does he even know about that?" I thought Fair and I were the only ones who knew about Scarlet and Lechatelierite's illegal romance. "How does he even know you served in the Diving Fleet? You said the Trilateral Committee kept you out of the media."

Scarlet threw her hands up. "Apparently, he knows more than the Trilateral Committee, because breaking the Laws of Emotional Protection isn't one of Cease's charges."

"What *are* they charging him with, anyway? And, why does everyone think he's going mad?" *Going* mad. Right. The man already was a total psycho; Scarlet was just too smitten to see it.

"Does it matter?" Fair seethed. "Enough on this topic! Enough! I've had it up to *here* with Cease Lechatelierite!"

I looked at her, pieces falling into place. "Does one of Cease's charges involve you?"

"If you must know, Ambrek, yes! And, though I know the alliance needs Cease, I'm actually glad he's getting what he deserves, okay?"

Scarlet gave Fair a scandalized stare.

"Don't start defending him again!" Fair reeled before Scarlet could say a word. "Whenever the topic comes up, you always say the same, stupid thing: 'I told you he's changed! You didn't let him apologize!'" she mocked Scarlet's high-pitched plea. "Let's just settle this once and for all, Scarlet: no, I still haven't forgiven him, and no, I don't think you should hold your breath, because Ichthyosis will melt in hell before I do!"

Scarlet took a step forward, green gaze venomous. If she still had her eye fire, Fair would be a pile of ashes on the floor.

"Hey!" I jumped between them. "Hey, alright, ladies! Let's calm down and get down to business, shall we?

Plan 'B' is now on the table. Let's brainstorm: how may we go about infiltrating a sea battle? I'll get the ball rolling and give you a little update: while you two were away, I went with a few men from Sixth Cabin to the Mage Castle for some snooping on the System's sea battle schedule. I didn't tell them why I needed the intel, so don't worry—they're still perfectly ignorant about the crystal."

Scarlet considered the crystal's existence as sensitive intel. Classified. Scarlet doubted her excitable, leap-be-fore-looking comrades would be able to contain such in-flammatory information without word reaching the System, which would then trigger a rat race. If the shard's existence became public knowledge, she said, it'd cause widespread pandemonium and panic. As for me, I didn't tell the System about it because I didn't want to share the glory of the return of the spectral web with anyone else. So, right now, only Scarlet, Fair and myself knew about the stone in the sea, and I wanted to keep it that way until I actually retrieved the thing and tossed it into the Fire Pit.

"Anyway, to put a long story short," I went on, "we found out the System is planning on launching their next na-val offensive against Ichthyosis on January seventh. I've also determined who'd be best to kidnap and replace—pi-lot Cu Twentnine and his co-pilot Rusty Pypes, a pair of low-ranking seabed scavengers." Since Conflagria didn't have a single natural metal mine, the System appointed men to scout for ship debris during battles, to bring home for recycling. "Scavengers fly convertible vessels, because they're responsible for transporting their loot to the Mage Castle, post-combat. So, we'll have a good sub-plane at our disposition. Plus, the System has finally learned to dupli-cate the Nordic's pressure-resistant, 'arrhythmic' fabric and internal suit-heaters, and intend to properly outfit every soldier by the time of dispatch."

"The System analyzed their stolen goods and consequently made a huge advancement in the world of high-tech warfare," Fair murmured. "Goody."

"I'm not thrilled either," I lied, "but, you've got to admit, the timing is perfect—this really works to our advantage."

Fair nodded. "Yeah."

"We've only got five days," I continued, "so, we've got to act fast and—"

"Wow, slow down, Ambrek." Scarlet put up her hands. "Were you *expecting* my meeting in Alcove City to go up in flames, or what?"

I blinked. "No, of course not. I thought the Nurian businessmen would cooperate."

Scarlet studied my face. "So, in the last couple days, you implemented, recruited the manpower for, and successfully executed a complex spy mission more dangerous than trying to steal Principal Tincture's robe off his back." Well, my lie sure smelled fishy when put like *that*. "Why would you go through the trouble? Moreover, why would you ask Sixth Cabin to? I thought we agreed on no more infiltrations, since we can't seem to pull one off without heavy losses."

My palms were sweaty. My palms didn't do that sort of thing when I had my hand-magic. "I, um, just thought I'd use our time wisely while you were gone and, you know, look into my backup plan, just in case."

"Look into it? We're talking about serious espionage. We're talking about throwing our men far behind enemy lines. That isn't something we just ask comrades to do, *in case*. That's a cautious, last-resort move. You should've waited to hear how my meeting with Cease's dad went, first. What if we succeeded and your crazy mission was all for naught? Someone could've died! In vain!"

"I...sorry." I was handing Scarlet everything she needed on a silver platter—valuable intel about the System and a golden plan to get the crystal—and she had the nerve to be upset?

"*Did* anyone get hurt or killed?" she pressed.

"No." Because there *was* no mission. I was just relaying news from Anapes.

"Are you sure?"

"Not a hair fell from a Red's head, Scarlet, I promise."

"How did you pull that off? Every time we've infiltrated the Castle, there's been bloodshed."

Fair waved her hand. "Never mind that now, Scarlet, I want to hear the rest of Ambrek's update."

I felt a rush of gratitude toward Fair. Fair may've been hotheaded and annoying as hell, but she wasn't the type to get all riled up over risking our warriors' lives…in a war.

I went on: "The System intends to keep this battle in the Septentrion Sea, so we'll have to slip away and travel pretty far, to get to the southern rim of the Briny Ocean—"

"The fragment won't be there, anymore," Fair interjected. "Scarlet and I saw a Nurian weather broadcast while we were in the city. Apparently, the earthquake caused a northbound tsunami that swept across the three seas, reportedly carrying debris from the carrier Cease crashed into the Fervor Base all the way to the Ichthyothian shore."

Scarlet looked pensive. "You know, I never did find out how Cease managed to survive that crash."

There was a tense pause.

"Because of me," Fair answered, voice low. "He fell through his windshield, unconscious, and I caught him with my hair, because I wanted to take him captive." And, she was the one who wound up as *his* prisoner. How did Cease manage that?

Scarlet's brows shot to her hairline.

As valuable as Cease was to the Ichthyothian Resistance, Fair clearly resented saving his life. I wondered for

the umpteenth time what he did to her during that interrogation. It was *some* company Scarlet kept. She spent every day with two people who abhorred the man she loved.

If Fair hadn't caught Cease, Crimson would still be breathing
and the spectrum wouldn't have diffused. It was amazing, how
one man could turn the whole world upside-down.

"Anyway," Fair continued, "I don't really understand all
that meteorological stuff they said, but the bottom line is,
we can assume the crystal got swept up north, too."

I rubbed my hands together. "Alright, so there are pros
and cons to that." Con: the shard was now at the enemy's
backdoor. "Pro: since we'll already be in the Septentrion
Sea for the battle, we won't have to waste tons of time and
fuel traveling thousands of miles just to *begin* our search."

"That's a pretty big pro," Fair commented.

"Con: we can't just take the ship and fly away; we'll have
to stay and search, right under everyone's noses," Scarlet said.

"Con," I said, "we'll be with the System Water Forces,
right in the thick of things, which means we'll be at risk of
Ichthyothian attack."

Scarlet moaned.

"We'll have our own weapons systems, though," I pointed
out, "so, it's not like we wouldn't be able to defend ourselves."

Scarlet stared at me, horrified.

"Alright, onto the next order of business," I plowed on,
before she could start whining about the immorality of
shooting at our dear 'friends,' the Nordics. "*Our* offensive."

"What are you talking about?" Scarlet asked.

"We're going to get our hands on a convertible, right?"
I said. "We might-as-well use it for all its worth. After we
grab the crystal and hightail out of the sea, why not do a
flyby over the Mage Castle and bomb it to pieces?"

Two jaws unhinged.

"What?" Fair gaped.

"Come on," I said, "why just grab the crystal and run? Rusty and Cu will be expected to deliver their loot to the Mage Castle, after the battle. So, let's go to the Mage Castle. But, instead of parking, we could fly overhead and blow it up. It'll be after hours, by then, so school will be out; there won't be any kids inside, anymore. Just System administration. We could kill Tincture."

Scarlet blinked. "That's a great idea, Ambrek. There's just one little problem."

"What's that?"

"We don't have a bomb," she answered dryly.

"Now it's your turn to stop thinking like a Nordic." I spread my arms. "We can make one. Come on, Fair, didn't you design the Underwater Fire? Would a firebomb be much different?"

Fair's face deepened as Scarlet gawked at her. It must've been hard for Scarlet to hear her best friend was the inventor of the System's greatest spectral weapon. The very weapon that wiped out dozens of her former Nordic comrades. The very weapon that nearly killed Cease during that infamous battle, an age and a half ago.

"Yes, it would," Scarlet finally answered. "Knowledge of spectroscopy and electromagnetism won't help us make a weapon powerful enough to wipe out a massive, stone fortress. That'd require chemistry and physics."

"It took until the mid-eighteen-hundreds for First Earth to manufacture their first air bombs," Fair said. "We've been without magic for, what, five months? We still haven't figured out the whole running-water thing. I wouldn't know where to begin, with something like this."

"No one in the Red ranks knows any chemistry or physics?" Come on, Scarlet.

"Well, I do," she piped, right on cue. Atta girl. "Of course, my memory is no longer perfect, so a lot of what I learned is fuzzy, by now. But, I guess I can try to figure things out."

"Great." I said, jump and she said, how high?

"And, I think you're right that, of all bombs, an incendiary would make the most sense, since Conflagria has petroleum and gelling agents, to make napalm. Plus, a firebomb would be small, light and easy to transport. Getting the metal for it will be tough, though. The exterior is supposed to be…aluminum, iron oxide or magnesium, if I remember correctly."

Pre-diffusion, the System had no need to steal warships from Nuria—they made their own from wood, spectrally reinforced to withstand deep-sea submersion and enemy fire as well as any metal. Lack of metal was the main reason the System was yet to copy the Nurians and build their own high-tech vessels from scratch. Seafloor scavengers like Cu Twentnine and Rusty Pypes never salvaged enough for entirely new constructions—their loot was only sufficient for repairing damage done to the tech-ships we already stole. But, Tincture and Anapes were the ones who sanctioned the bomb project and asked me to use Scarlet's genius to make it happen. So, they were more than willing to spare the metal the Reds would need for it. Scarlet and her men just couldn't know the resources were being voluntarily handed to them by their enemy.

"Don't worry about that," I said. "While the folks from Sixth Cabin and I were poking around the Mage Castle yesterday, we stole a scrap of vitreous silica wing."

"You already have the metals?" Scarlet asked, faintly. "For Tincture's sake, does my presence stifle your productivity or something?"

"N-no."

"And, you're *sure* no one died on your mission?"

"Yes!"

"Where's the metal, now?" Fair cut in, to my relief.

"Seventh Cabin." Seventh was the closest Red strong-hold to the Mage Castle. Anapes had a couple of his men leave the wing fragment on Seventh's doorstep, in the middle of the night. I imagined, though the Reds had no idea where it came from, they were beyond thrilled to receive such a precious commodity.

"I hope that hunk of vitreous silica isn't from a recent battle," Scarlet whimpered, disgustingly worried for her dear Nordics.

"I wouldn't know," I said. It felt good to answer at least one question honestly. Anapes didn't bother to enlighten me with that kind of detail.

"If I had to guess, it's probably from when Cease crashed into the Fervor Sea Base," said Fair. "Getting a crap-load of metal was the one silver lining to that whole mess. Though, the System didn't have nearly as much need for it, pre-diffusion, since spectrally-reinforced wood worked well enough. I imagine they're grateful for it, now, though."

"As grateful as they could be, all things considered," I muttered. That crash was the reason Cease turned up on base. The reason he was at the right time and place to kill my sister.

Scarlet noticed the agony in my voice and put an arm around me. She stroked my shoulder gently, sweet melancholy in her eyes. To the Reds and the Nordics, Crimson Cerise was the face of an evil dictatorship. To them, her death was a major triumph. And, yet, I got the Red Leader herself to feel pain over Crimson's loss, because she genuinely cared for and sympathized with me. I smiled internally. I had Scarlet eating out of the palm of my hand.

Though, since I failed to turn our relationship romantic, I was yet to *fully* take Lechatelierite's domineering place in her psyche. Even locked up in a jail cell fifteen-hundred miles away, Lechatelierite was still foiling my plans. But, my advance on Scarlet wasn't a total bust. I got her to admit she loved me. I got her to start seeing me in a sexual light. I gave her a tempting taste of our chemistry. And, from the way she looked at me and often found excuses to casually embrace or touch me, I could tell she was daily toying with the idea of loving me the way she loved her ex-commander. She wasn't so hands-on with anyone else in the Red ranks.

"Alright, well," Scarlet said, withdrawing her arm, cheeks slightly pinker than usual. "Vitreous silica wings are made of a whole bunch of alloys, so we'd need to melt that piece down into individual elements before we can do anything with it. Fair, could you ask Prunus and his men to take care of that?"

"Sure."

Scarlet took a deep breath. "Five days."

"Five days to design and construct what took First Earth eras," Fair murmured.

"Isn't 'century' the First Earth word for 'era'?" I asked. "I think 'era' meant something else, to them."

Fair rolled her eyes. "Whatever. Five days to do what took First Earth *centuries.*"

I reached forward and boldly took Scarlet's warm, tiny hand in mine. "If anyone can pull off something like that, it's you. Just let us know what we can do to help. We're at your service."

Scarlet smiled, and the beauty of it stabbed me in the chest.

"Thanks, Ambrek. You're the best."

SCARLET JULY

I squinted at the page. Even after five months, it felt odd to squint for the purpose of seeing more clearly, especially when the object in question was only inches away.

Working on Ambrek's bomb, I buried my nose in parchment, filling scroll after scroll with chemical equations, formulas and diagrams. I worked through throbbing headaches—pain shot through my scalp and eyes—as my body silently pined for spectrum, for the swell of energy that'd alleviate my aching muscles, remove the blinders from my eyes and lift the invisible weights from my limp hair. Before ending the Crystal, I didn't anticipate how awful it'd be to live without magic. I figured, if most of Second Earth lived like that, we mages could adapt. Infrared frequencies would feel like the 'new normal' in no time, right? Wrong. Living without an aura was like being sick. It was like decaying alive. No wonder the System-supporters movement was so strong, these days. I doubted anyone really agreed with the idea of spectral mind-control—except the controllers themselves, of course—but a whole lot of people were, understandably, upset over losing their magic, thirsting for revenge against the one who 'stole' it.

If only the spectral web and the System's thought-control weren't a packaged deal.

Diffused, I no longer had an eidetic memory. Five months ago, this project would've been a breeze. But now, it was a real strain to recall stuff I read up to six-and-a-half ages ago. There certainly weren't any relevant references here in Conflagria to consult; we just had a whole lot of useless spectroscopy texts and color wheels. And, history books. I thought some of the resources on First Earth history might help, but those only served to remind me how the First Earthlings *used* firebombs in their wars, not how they made them.

As I worked, it was hard not to stress. Not only was I racing against the sundial toward the January seventh deadline, I knew if I messed up on a single calculation, the entire project could literally self-destruct.

At first, Fair insisted on 'helping' me, peering over my shoulder and making rather unhelpful remarks.

$$6C_{10}H_{15}O_7 + heat \rightarrow 10CH_2O + C_{50}H_{10}O$$
$$CH_2O + air \rightarrow CO_2 + mH_2O + nCO + pC + qN_2$$

"'Cho'?" Fair asked, blankly. "What's 'cho'?"

Having spent about thirty minutes on those two lines alone, I wasn't in a very patient or understanding mood.

"It's not 'cho,' Fair. 'C,' 'H' and 'O' are the chemical symbols for carbon, hydrogen and oxygen," I snapped. "When an ignition source heats wood to about five-hundred degrees, the cellulose in the *wood*," I pointed to the first term in the equation, "decomposes and yields *volatile gases* and *char*." I pointed, in turn, to the terms after the arrow.

"But, Scarlet, the Mage Castle is made of stone, not wood."

"Well, I have to start somewhere!" I burst, elbow sending Ambrek's ink jar to the floor.

Fair took a step back. "Tincture, Scarlet, I'm only trying to help."

"Well, then, you can stop sitting around like a Useless and go find something productive to do!"

"Alright, fine." She stood. "No need to get all Cease-ish at me." And, she turned on her heel and stalked out the door, not even bothering to pitch in with cleaning up the mess, first.

My hands, feet and face felt prickly-numb with cold. But, somehow, I was also sweating. Icy beads rolled down my back. Panting, I caught sight of my reflection in the murky puddle of ink. My skin was unusually white. There was no trace of my normal flush.

Grunting, I got up and kicked the broken bottle on the floor. A chunk of glass flew through the air...and hit Ambrek, standing in the doorway.

He blinked. "Scarlet, is everything alright?"

I bit my lip so hard it bled.

Without my asking, Ambrek pulled out his handkerchief, stooped and started wiping. When I squatted beside him to help, he caught my shoulder.

"No, no, I'll take care of this. Just sit back. Relax."

I leaned against the wall, knees folded, inexplicable rage lingering in my chest. I took a deep breath and scrunched my lids shut, for a moment.

Once Ambrek was done, he scooted beside me. "What's going on, Scarlet? Talk to me. Are you having a tough time with the project?"

I nodded.

He dropped the soggy rag and took my icy hands in his large, warm, ink-smeared ones. "I'm really sorry for putting this crazy burden on you."

I looked into his serene eyes and felt my anger begin to ebb.

"Don't be. I can do it. I will."

"Are you feeling okay?" He squeezed my frozen fingers. "You're so pale and cold."

"I'm fine," I lied.

"I ran into Fair outside. She said, 'enter at your own risk.' Did you guys have a fight or something?"

I looked at my sandals, embarrassed. "I don't know what came over me. Fair was just trying to help, and I yelled and threw her out."

Ambrek patted my shoulder. "It's hard to be yourself when under this much pressure."

I definitely didn't feel like myself. Frustration at a time like this was understandable. But, unbearable surges of white-hot rage certainly weren't. It was almost like someone else's aura was inside of me or something.

"You should've seen me, the night before my Circle Trial," Ambrek went on, chuckling. "I punched a hole through my bedroom wall, when my sister was just playfully teasing me about being a 'two-toned freak show.' Not my finest moment."

I smiled back. Just a couple minutes with Ambrek, and I was feeling better already.

"Yeah, well, it's easy for hand mages to accidentally do things like that. And, you were a kid. I had a short fuse too, when I was little."

Ambrek playfully poked me in the rib. "You're still little."

"I thought I outgrew my temper and learned some discipline in the Diving Fleet. But, I guess the transformation wasn't as complete as I hoped."

My flip-out at Fair reminded me a lot of Cease, and not the parts I liked. I remembered how my mood and self-perception oscillated with his ever-changing attitude toward me. I remembered our long nights in his quarters, drawing up battle plans, feeling the pressure of the perfection he expected, dreading the possibility of letting him down and setting him off. Working with him was an emotional, roller-coaster ride. When mad, he didn't resort to crude words or schoolkid insults, like Amok Kempt. He wielded his intelligence and keen understanding of your psyche to really hit you where it hurt. He'd critique and criticize in a chilly, paralyzing tone that'd make the strongest of soldiers wish to evaporate into thin air. When he blew up, his throat-mage-like voice was like a flaming sword in the ear. He also was liable to pound his fist on tables, kick things, throw things, grab your collar and yell right in your face, and even strike you to the floor. The memories made me shudder. I loved Cease, but he had a dark side I really didn't miss.

Ambrek started squeezing the tension from my shoulders. "How about you take a break for a bit and spend some time going over pilotry basics with me?" he asked, voice mellow and sweet.

"Sure."

We anticipated Pypes and Twentnine's sub would be identical—or, fairly similar, at least—to the Ichthyothian scouts I'd flown before, since most tech warships in the northwestern hemisphere were all made by the same company—Cease's dad's. So, last night, I sketched up some console diagrams for Ambrek to study. As if the incendiary project weren't stressful enough, I had four days to teach Ambrek how to fly without an actual craft to practice on. At least, on the seventh, he wouldn't be deploying alone; I'd be there to help.

As the three of us hammered out the details of the mission last night, Fair initially got pretty upset when Ambrek and I decided she wouldn't be heading out to sea with us. We only needed two pilots—one for each navigation and weaponry. Ambrek had to go because he knew who to kidnap and I had to go because finding the crystal required my sense of awareness and, when in range, eye spectrum. Ambrek would take care of navigation, freeing me to focus on staring at the seafloor.

So, Fair would stay behind with the System pilots we abducted. Unlike Ambrek and I, Fair actually had experience with detaining POWs; she held Inexor for nearly an age. The only POW I ever dealt with was… well, her. And, I didn't exactly do a good job with her, either. Looking back, I wished I'd done something to stop Cease from abusing her the way he did. But, I was too afraid to stand against him. I was a coward.

Anyway, Fair only accepted her unglamorous assignment after Ambrek reasoned with her for a while. A long while. I was amazed by his patience. Ambrek was gifted at persuasion and ameliorating awkward, interpersonal situations, which the Reds—a rather boisterous bunch—had no shortage of. I often felt Ambrek was the glue that kept the revolution together.

As I sat with him now, detailing the semantics of take-offs and landings and explaining every dial, button, knob and lever on the diagram I'd sketched, I was thoroughly impressed with how quickly he seemed to be absorbing everything. He needed little to no repetition on my part, anticipating correct answers to tough questions.

"Tincture, Ambrek, if I didn't know any better, I'd say you already know how to pilot!" I laughed. This was great. Getting Ambrek sea-battle-ready by the seventh had me worried sick, but it looked like I'd been fretting over nothing. He was a natural. And, the less time I needed to spend on being his instructor, the more time I could spend on the incendiary.

Ambrek shrugged, oddly unenthusiastic about my praise. "I did *just* see some System pilots in action, after all."

"Well, then, I'm grateful the System is so stupid about security. I'd never hold a POW where they can see what I'm doing and learn to fly my ship. What, did they keep you in the cockpit or something?"

He just shrugged, again. Ambrek didn't like to talk much about his captivity. He was still yet to share exactly how he used his hand-magic to escape. He tended to clam up, whenever I asked him. Not that I blamed him. I imagined the whole ordeal was traumatic for him, especially since he was still relatively new to the world of war. I figured, he'd open up when he was ready.

The next few days were like one long, feverish spell. Fair stayed at Seventh Cabin with Prunus and his team, so it was just Ambrek and I. Ambrek checked up on me obsessively, bringing me water, dragon meat, taro-root and fire, without my asking. Every few hours, he suggested I take a quick break with him, strolling outside or sitting for another back massage or answering more questions about pilotry. Most of the time, he just sat beside me as I scribbled away, studying and keeping me company. The equations just seemed to flow more smoothly from my quill when he was around. Whenever I got stuck, Ambrek would ask what the problem was and offer ludicrous suggestions that never solved anything, but made me laugh and unwind enough to quickly crack back down.

Whenever he took a peek at my work, I couldn't help but remember the way my stomach knotted up whenever Cease towered over my desk. A couple times, when I looked up at Ambrek, I half-expected to see Cease's stern, silver glare instead of Ambrek's warm, gold gaze.

One night, Ambrek disappeared for hours. I wouldn't have noticed if I weren't staying up late to work on the bomb. But, I was too preoccupied to ask him where he was off to. He hadn't adjusted to the thirty-six-hour days yet, so I figured he was just coping with insomnia by taking a walk on the beach or something. He had a right to some personal time without being interrogated about it, anyway. It was easy to let the revolution consume your identity and sanity.

If Ambrek needed a moment alone to clear his head, away from me and the incendiary project, he deserved it. Just as Fair deserved to spend a few days away from Headquarters, with Prunus. She, like all my hardworking Reds, needed a little pleasure—or, at least normalcy—once in a while.

Normalcy. What did that word even mean, anymore? What would my life be like now, if I were a so-called 'normal' sixteen-age-old mage? If I were born with only one source? If I were never declared Useless and exiled? If I never learned about the Ichthyo-Conflagrian War, enlisted in the Diving Fleet, met Cease, destroyed the Crystal and started a civil war? What did regular, non-Useless, Conflagrian girls do, before the diffusion? Some of them were still warriors. Fair Gabardine and Crimson Cerise were asked to serve in the Water Forces while in their teen ages. But, they were the exception, not the rule. Pre-diffusion, most young, female mages didn't lead a soldier's life. So, I probably never would've learned to kill. I never would've had to watch a man die, feeling a part of myself die in solidarity. I probably would've been assigned to a scholarly profession, like spectroscopy. And, I'd probably be with my betrothed by now, whoever he was—I was deported before I was old enough to find out. I'd be married and maybe even a mother. In Nordic culture, people tended to wait until their twenties or thirties to settle down. But, here, it was normal for girls to marry and start a family before reaching their second decade.

I wondered if I would've been content with the life of a wife, mother and spectroscoper. Cooking and keeping house and raising children and studying electromagnetism. I wondered if my heart would've been happy with an arranged marriage. I couldn't imagine another man stirring the same fire Cease awakened in me. But, I supposed, if I never met Cease, I wouldn't have grounds for comparison.

Knowing nothing else, I probably would've taught my heart to quietly love the life and the husband assigned to me.

Since leaving the Diving Fleet, I had no personal ambitions. I had plenty for my country and for Second Earth, but none for myself. I wanted to see Conflagria freed of the System's oppression, peaceful and democratic. I wanted to see the Ichthyo-Conflagrian War resolved, the northwest relieved of the threat of imperialism. I wanted to see Second Earth abolish its cold isolationism. These were all worthy dreams to have. But, none of them were about *me*. And, that definitely wasn't normal. Most people didn't aspire to save the world in their lifetimes. Most people just wanted a job they enjoyed or at least tolerated, food on the table, and friends and family to walk alongside. But, I didn't think about my own future, just that of my country and my planet. Because, if the System squashed the Red Revolution and the Nurro-Ichthyothian Resistance, none of us would have any future, at all. So, I had no choice but to put my own life on hold as long as the world was in shambles. I absolutely had to die to myself, committing my body, mind and soul to dreams that were larger than me. Right?

To be honest, I wasn't totally sure the wisest answer was yes. Before we met, Cease lived for nothing but the Ichthyothian Resistance. He had no life beyond his duty, no diversity of thought or ambition beyond what the Childhood Program taught or the Trilateral Committee allowed. He cared for nothing and no one else but the war. And, I was appalled by that. I thought that mindset and lifestyle were oppressive and dehumanizing. I thought the Trilateral Committee committed a grievous crime by forcing entire generations to live like that. Well, what was the difference between my life now and that of the base-raised divers? The civil war wasn't just my job, it was what I ate, slept and breathed. I gave no mind to pleasure, friendship or hobbies.

I hadn't sketched for fun since that fateful review class at Icicle, when I inadvertently gave Cease the idea to attack the Fervor Sea Base. I hadn't taken a single swim in the Fervor River—my favorite childhood pastime—since coming home in August. I hadn't held a real, relaxed, non-work-related conversation with anyone since my sleepless nights in the Diving Fleet barracks, when I still bunked with Nurtic Leavesleft. I wanted so much more for Cease and his comrades than the ascetic life they were forced into. Yet, three-thousand miles away from Icicle, I was choosing to lead my own life no differently.

Most of my fellow Reds made time for themselves, even in the midst of the chaos and strife. Since returning to the island, I saw young mages marry. I saw couples have kids. I saw birthday parties and the annual Vernal Equinox Day celebration. I saw families fly kites and build sandcastles on the beach. I saw groups of friends huddle by bonfires, singing and roasting dragon meat. I saw Fair and Prunus flirt and laugh and race their scabrouses down the paths.

I saw Ambrek profess his love for me. I felt his arms around my body and his kiss on my lips. Even Ambrek, wholeheartedly dedicated to the Red cause, wasn't content to wait until all was right with the world before pursuing something for himself—not his army, not his country, but just himself. Me.

But, I couldn't give Ambrek what he wanted. I couldn't give him my heart. It's not that I didn't care for him. It's not that I wasn't attracted to him. It's not that he didn't possess qualities any woman would want. Ambrek really was the complete package. From a strictly logical perspective, there were many ways Ambrek was actually a better fit for me than Cease. He shared my same cultural and ethnic background. He was even-keel and considerate. He seemed naturally attentive to my needs, accommodating them without my asking. He was already in tune with his heart and emotions, before we met. He didn't need to endure significant trauma to learn to love.

Cease had to learn from ground zero. He came from a highly-dysfunctional background and would likely struggle with his humanity to some degree for the rest of his life. He had callouses and scars all over his heart. He was the type of person capable of torturing a teenage girl until she begged for death at his feet. He had somewhat of a soft interior, but it was encased in an iron fortress, miles thick. He had a volatile temper, an argumentative nature, and a dark side I suspected I only caught a glimpse of.

But, Cease was Cease. And, that was all he needed to be, to win my heart. I didn't love him just because he was the most brilliant, brave, strong, talented and selfless person I ever met. I didn't love him just because he proved he cared more for me than the war he believed he was born for. I didn't love him just because our chemistry was insane and his electric kisses haunted me every single day since I tasted them. Or, because I found his pinched face, deathly pallor, wild hair, hypnotic voice, paralyzing stare and much-too-lean build even more attractive than Ambrek's conventionally-handsome bulk, bronze tan, gentle smile and warm eyes. I loved Cease because he was the beautiful disaster that he was. It didn't have to make logical sense.

And so, my heart wasn't free for the taking. Because, even after five months, it was still too raw and broken over leaving Cease so suddenly. It was stupid, I knew that. I was a fool to push away someone like Ambrek in favor of a fading memory. But, my mind couldn't force my heart to take that leap.

Not yet, anyway.

* * *

The Reds stayed on the defensive since the incendiary project began. For the most part, the System also stayed quiet. Their inaction was unusual, but we sure weren't complaining.

Tonight, I was barely an inch from the finish-line, and my nerves were rigged with anxiety. Still accustomed to mechanical pencils over quills, I awkwardly blotted and smeared ink all over the parchment, numbers and lines swimming before my eyes...

"Scarlet!" Someone shook my shoulder, roughly. "Scarlet, that's enough for tonight. You're falling asleep on the page!"

Familiar words. I'd heard them before.

My snapped up. "I'm sorry, sir!"

"Did you just speak Ichthyothian...and call me, sir?"

I blinked my eyes stupidly and looked over my shoulder...at Ambrek.

"You," I blurted.

"That's it. You're going to bed, right now, whether you like it or not." He rolled up my scroll and tucked it into his robe. "I'm returning this to you tomorrow morning, and not bloody well until then. There's seven hours until dawn. Sleep."

I felt a rush of gratitude toward Ambrek. I wanted to put down the final strokes, but sleep sounded much more appealing. Sleep. A full night of it! Obediently, I got up from the table, wobbled to my room and tumbled into my tarp.

CEASE LECHATELIERITE

It was thirty-two o'clock. One hour left until dinner. In the quarry, it was too loud to hear your own grunting, so, at the end of each day, we were signaled to reconvene by the vibrations of our ankle-monitors.

Of course, inmates weren't permitted to operate heavy machinery or explosives, so we stayed near the rim, carving with mallets and wedges. January was supposed to be the coldest month of the age, but apparently, in southern Nuria, that meant the temperature hovered between thirty to forty degrees. So, in the quarry, it was fifty to sixty. As I worked, sweat trickled down my hair and face, tickling my earplugs and creeping under my visual band. My prison jumpsuit—dark orange, like the uniforms of the System Water Forces—clung to my body like a diving suit, waterlogged with perspiration. In the near-distance, the channelers of my father's company swung wrecking balls and ignited dynamite. The flashes of light, thunderous rumbles and suffocating heat reminded me of the Conflagrian Fire Pit.

I struck wedge after wedge, thoughts swirling around my head like a typhoon. I thought about my forthcoming court-martial and how the fate of the northwestern hemisphere hung in the balance. I thought about the mystery of the spectral web's intermittent crystallization and wondered if there was, in fact, something in the sea causing it as Nurtic Leavesleft suggested. I thought about my fleet and wondered how Leavesleft was holding up, in my place. I thought about my vision of Scarlet's inexplicable betrayal. And, despite my fury toward Scarlet, I couldn't help but think about August seventh, as I did every day since. I thought about our farewell. About how warm and soft Scarlet's lips felt on mine. About how passionately she kissed me back, how electric her body felt in my arms, how cute she looked standing on her toes to reach me better. About how hard it was to stop, how the way she clung to me just encouraged me to continue, how the only reason I had to pull away at some point was because I was afraid Nurtic Leavesleft and Fair Gabardine would walk in. When I made the first move, Scarlet seemed nervous for a moment, but she got over that quickly enough, eagerly moving her lips with mine.

When the System pilot kissed her, she didn't respond like that. There was no fire in her reaction. She just stood there and took it. And, she squirmed and turned her head after only one kiss. Maybe I was grasping at straws here, but Scarlet's body language toward the pilot gave me the impression she wasn't all in.

Yet, my heart still ached. Because, I knew how Scarlet would react to a *truly* unwanted advance. She wouldn't just endure it, she'd fight back. Violently. When Amok Kempt kissed her, she set his sleeve on fire and ran for her life. So, while she may not have been the most eager recipient of the System pilot's affections, she didn't exactly despise him, either. She didn't recoil or push him away or retaliate. She let him hold her. She let him finish the kiss. She looked up at him with sweetness in her eyes. She pressed her cheek to his chest. She clearly cared about this man and didn't want to hurt him.

I heaved my mallet over my shoulder, about to take another swing, when something knocked me square in the back, sending me on a wild tumble into the rocky cavern, visual band flying off my face. I fell as though dropping from a vitreous silica, the choppy surface of the sea rushing up at me—

AMOK KEMPT

Lechatelierite didn't make a sound as he fell to his likely death. If not death, I figured he'd at least break his neck and get paralyzed, again—hopefully, for good, this time.

I hated him for taking the war from me. I saw the way he always used to look at Scarlet—possessively, hungrily, lustfully—and I supposed he wanted to eliminate anyone likely to get to her first. So, instead of slapping me on the wrist, he actually reported me to the Trilateral Committee and had me court-martialed. He was the reason I was stuck in this sewer.

Since we first met, Lechatelierite was an arrogant, power-hungry despot. At ten ages old, he was a scrawny little runt with an attitude, too full of himself for food. At sixteen, I was the sub-leader of his unit. It was unnerving, to take orders from a little kid who acted like a seasoned vet of decades. Despite his obvious brilliance, I couldn't stand being under his thumb. So, I got a couple of our comrades to tamper with his helmet before his first sea battle, hoping hypothermia or water pressure would take care of him. But, somehow, Lechatelierite not only survived the conflict, but got Sutreppoc iced and Kerbma asphyxiated.

Well, he wasn't getting away, this time.

I turned my back on the pit and began climbing up to the rim. After about twenty minutes, I felt a hand seize me around the neck and, the next thing I knew, my head was hitting rock.

Colors spun before my eyes as I rolled over. Spread-eagled on my back, I felt something grab my collar and shake me. Slowly, the fog cleared, revealing the deathly-white face and silver-grey glare of Cease Lechatelierite. An inexplicable mist, black as the night sky, seemed to hover around him. His jumpsuit was ripped all over, exposed skin bruised and cut. How did he survive the fall? Moreover, how was he well enough to hike all the way back up here, especially so quickly?

Lips by my ear, he spoke in a low, menacing tone, "This isn't about you or me or Scarlet July. This is about Ichthyosis. This is about the war. My court-martial is on the seventh, and if there's a chance I'll be allowed to return to duty, I need to be around to take it. Ichthyosis *needs* me, dammit, and if there's a single drop of soldier blood left in you, you'd realize what you tried to do just now is the equivalent of waving a white flag before the System."

With that, he released his iron grip and stalked away, leaving me, immobilized and concussed, on the hot stone.

NURTIC LEAVESLEFT

I strained in my seat, peering out the windshield of my crystalline.

"Units seven and eight, deploy from the vitreous silica. Crystallines two and three, protective gyrate," I ordered.

Much to the annoyance of the base-raised, I spoke Nurian during practice, and likewise planned to in battle. It was either that or leave the majority of my men in the dark. The Nurro-Ichthyothian Diving Fleet was disproportionately heavy on the 'Nurro.' My nation gave Ichthyosis everything—resources, materiel, manpower—yet, Ichthyosis didn't seem the slightest bit grateful. Nuria's southern ports were ransacked by the System often, yet the Trilateral Committee—ever out of touch with reality—still wouldn't let me spare a single unit for their protection.

It was true, my fellow Nurian comrades tended not to be as gifted in warfare as the rigid Ichthyothians who grew up learning nothing but. It was true, we typically were the weaker links in the fleet. But, without us, the Diving Fleet wouldn't have enough links to be a real chain, at all. Without us, Ichthyosis would have no choice but to surrender.

Whether in the air or under the sea, I felt exhilarated and invigorated whenever I piloted. I absolutely loved to fly. But, something nagged the corner of my mind, whenever I sat in the cockpit of a warship. The orders that escaped my lips were always punctured with doubt. Every time I commanded another to kill or be killed, destroy or be destroyed, I felt a little sick inside. And, over the past five months, I slowly began to realize that the Nurro-Ichthyothian Diving Fleet wasn't what I was born for.

Yes, it was a beautiful thing to serve my country and our ally. No, I didn't regret my enlistment, not for a second. I knew I was meant to be here. But, only for a time. The military wouldn't be my lifelong career. After leaving the fleet, I wouldn't seek greener pastures or quieter waters, either; I'd head right back into the warzone, but as a different kind of soldier. I wanted to join my church's aviation ministry and provide humanitarian relief to one the most impoverished and misunderstood people groups in the world: Conflagrians.

Until then, I'd fulfill my duty as commander of the Nurro-Ichthyothian Diving Fleet. I'd try my best to walk in the boots of the greatest military leader in Second Earth history and salvage the alliance from the brink of defeat. I'd strive to forge unity between the disjointed nationalities. I'd lead my men against the cunning, creative minds of the very people I longed to live with and aid. I first realized I had a heart for the Conflagrian people when I learned who Scarlet July really was.

I thought of Scarlet, every day. I wondered how she was doing now, carrying her nation on her delicate shoulders. Lechatelierite believed she got killed in combat during a sandstorm, but the more I thought about it, the more I disagreed. From Lechatelierite's descriptions of his visions, I concluded the System pilot was probably at sea the same time Scarlet was in battle on the shore. Which meant, when the spectral web crystallized, her aura probably did, too—if anyone would be affected by the return of the spectrum, it was the Multi-Source Enchant, no matter the distance. And so, when the torch lit her hair on fire, her magic would save her from burning alive.

Relieved my friend probably didn't die a fiery death, decapitating the leadership of the Red Revolution while she was at it, I was excited to share my speculations with my men. But, when I did, they only looked at me with the same tired incredulity they did Lechatelierite when he told us about his visions, in the first place. Scarlet July was probably fine, they said, not because she miraculously survived a torch to the head but because that whole story was nothing but a figment of Lechatelierite's imagination to begin with.

I understood if the Ichthyothians could care less what I believed, but I was shocked they'd write off Lechatelierite so easily. If we couldn't trust the judgement of a man like him, could we trust anyone in this world?

INEXOR BUIRD

Nurtic Leavesleft, Nurian Lefty Extraordinaire, was probably the greatest pilot to set foot on Second Earth, but the blunt truth was, he was an ineffective leader. Sure, he was smart. Sure, he had ideas that were worthy of even Cease and Scarlet. That wasn't the problem. The problem was, he was...well...himself. We Ichthyothians didn't like him because he was the most Nurian Nurian we'd ever met—the polar opposite to Cease, the epitome of soldier, the masterpiece of the Childhood Program. The Nurians loved Leavesleft and were proud of him, but they didn't take him seriously, treating him like a buddy rather than a chief. And, he encouraged their behavior by 'hanging out' with everyone during off-hours and condoning stupid shenanigans that undermined his authority. Maybe once or twice during his commandership, Cease sat with us in the rec room, after hours. Cease never came to the barracks or participated in banter of any sort, even during meals—if he opened his mouth in the mess hall, it was to discuss work. Unless we were actually in practice or battle, Cease tended to keep his distance from us, like a true professional. It was ludicrous to even think of playing pranks on him. But, Leavesleft? Leavesleft was soft on his men, eager to please. A couple days ago, when he took off his utility belt and left it in his unlocked quarters, Dither Maine and Arrhyth Link snuck in and wrapped his entire spool of deadline

around his bible. It took Leavesleft two hours to sheer off
the wire without slicing up the leather.

"Why do you let them do this to you, Leavesleft?" I
asked him, that night.

He just shrugged, hazel eyes as mellow as his tone. "I'm
going to have a talk with them about it."

"A talk?"

"Yeah, right after dinner, in the barracks," he answered.

Cease wouldn't have waited until after dinner, and he
wouldn't have met the perpetrators on their own turf.
He'd take one look at the book, hunt the culprits down,
scream their heads off with that sonic voice of his, drag
them out to sea without diving suits and make them wish
they never enlisted.

Cease ran a tight ship, but I never saw him use physical
force as a disciplinary tool, unlike his predecessor, the late
Ecrof Ecreoc. It was no secret Ecreoc and Cease weren't
fond of each other. Not long after promoting Cease to
second-in-command, Ecreoc realized he'd elevated a ri-
val. And, Cease disliked Ecreoc because he could hardly
bear to take orders from someone dumber than him. Cease
often emerged from Ecreoc's quarters with unexplained
bruises and cuts. Cease, being stoic and stubborn, got defensive whenever I tried to stick my nose in his business.
When Ecreoc died and Cease took his place, I was glad to
see Cease didn't turn around and do to his subordinates
what Ecreoc did to him. However, Illia Frappe told me he
witnessed Cease hitting a soldier, once. It happened while
I was still MIA. Cease struck Scarlet to the floor after
she tried to hug him in front of the entire fleet. The story
seemed so stupid, I thought Illia made it up. But, then I
read it in Cease's log. It was stunning, how Cease and Scarlet, a couple of the greatest geniuses on the planet, turned
into complete idiots when put together. I guessed it didn't

matter how smart you were, when it came to concerns of the heart. I could attest to that.

* * *

Tomorrow, January fifth, Icicle would receive its first, weekly status report of the ninety-fourth age, from Ground Troops Commander Slue and Air Force Commander Zephyr. This morning, Leavesleft, in nervous anticipation, ever-so-cordially asked me to take a look at it with him once it arrived.

"I think it'd be a good idea if we sit down sometime tomorrow and go through it together," he suggested carefully, as if it were a radically new concept, for fleet officers to collaborate over a war report. "Would that be alright with you?"

I fought the urge to scoff, or roll my eyes, or laugh, or do all three at once.

"Yes, Leavesleft, that's what we're supposed to do," I said, keeping the acid in my voice to a minimum. "And, then, we're supposed to write a reply."

Leavesleft looked alarmed, but he nodded vigorously and responded with a boisterous, "Yes, of course."

Cease, what the hell were you thinking when you promoted this buffoon? He was a nice guy. He was a great pilot. But, he was still nothing but a half-wit, Nurian rookie who didn't belong here. Him and his entire race.

AMBREK COPPERTUS

It was time. Time for the System to inform the Second Earth Order of the Nurro-Ichthyothian Alliance, enabling us to initiate a blockade.

In '1805' (Earth I, AD), during the Napoleonic Wars, France declared a blockade against Britain who then turned around and declared a blockade against all of continental Europe. But, turned out, neither country had the naval prowess to actually follow through; the true purpose behind these 'paper blockades' was to seize neutral passerby. This led to the erection of the three international principles of 'legal blockading' which were still upheld by the Second Earth Order today, to protect members from blacklisted, warring nations. The first and second laws mandated a blockade be 'formally declared' and 'effectively conducted.' The third law mandated all nearby neutral powers be given sufficient warning prior to the blockade's launch, allowing their ships sufficient time to exit hostile sea-space.

Today, for the first time since Conflagria's blacklisting four eras ago, the System would communicate directly with the Second Earth Order. In accordance with the first law, Conflagria would formally declare its siege against the illegal alliance. In accordance with the third law, we would give the Order until the night of the seventh to clear the Septentrion Sea of their rationing ships.

The stage was set.

INEXOR BUIRD

January fifth, seventeen o'clock.

Leavesleft was at the far left of the mess hall, in Cease's old spot, lanky figure hunched over the table. A trey of wheat crackers and a glass of ice water sat untouched, before him. His hazel eyes were wide as he perused what I assumed was the state-of-the-war report.

"Hey, Nurtic!" Dither Maine called as he exited the lunch line with a cup of yogurt.

Leavesleft didn't even lift his head.

Maine unceremoniously plunked down across from Leavesleft, stole a cracker from his plate and dipped it in his yogurt. I cringed. The Nurians were always making weird combinations with their food.

I remembered when, seven or so ages ago, the cooks decided to 'shake things up' by requesting a small shipment of some of the most popular Nurian foodstuffs. In came red paste and shriveled, oily, potato shreds, salty as the sea itself. Ketchup and fries. Beyond disgusting. I'd prefer the dragon giblets and rotten taro stems I was fed as a System POW. That was the last time the cafeteria attempted to serve fried products or pungent sauces.

About a month ago, Arrhyth Link was doing what Nurians did best and prowling where he didn't belong, when he found a forgotten canister of ketchup in a kitchen cabinet. The Nurian soldiers, who constantly complained of how 'plain' and 'boring' base food was, pounced on it like starving beggars. Never mind the tomato paste was long past its expiration; they consumed the entire supply in a matter of days. They put it on everything: crackers, rice, boiled potatoes, white bread, salmon—you named it, they ketchuped it.

"We wouldn't normally do this; we're just desperate," Link had reassured me then, when he saw the disgust on my face. "Usually, ketchup is just for things like burgers and fries." Like that explained anything.

Illia frowned. "I've tried fries before. They don't taste like potatoes. All you taste is salt and grease. They're so salty and soggy, it's like they've been dipped in hot seawater. I just don't understand why anyone would want to soak their food in a boiling vat of oil before eating it."

"Well, *I* don't understand why anyone would want to mash salmon into a paste and freezer-burn it before eating it," Link countered loudly. "And, I don't understand why anyone would want to eat everything stone-cold, straight from the fridge, as if the stove or the microwave haven't been invented yet."

Maine dropped a dollop of ketchup onto his bread. "Now, all this needs is some cheese and pepperoni, and we'd have pizza," he said dreamily.

"What's pepperoni?" I asked.

"What's pizza?" Illia asked.

And, they burst out laughing.

Until today, I still hadn't a clue what pizza was. Maine now stole another cracker from Leavesleft's plate. That was another strange thing Nurians often did: eat off each other's treys. Why not just get your own food from the serving line?

"Nurtic, are you deaf?" Maine waved his spoon at Leavesleft's face.

I approached Maine from behind. "Address your commander with some respect, soldier!" I barked in a loud, Cease-like voice.

He jumped in his seat. "Sir!"

"Go sit somewhere else; Leavesleft and I need to talk."

He nodded and scuttled away. I guessed he was going to have to get his own crackers, after all.

I sat down. "Sir." The word seemed to scratch my throat whenever I had to call Leavesleft that. "The disrespect you condone is—"

Wordlessly, he silenced me by handing over the packet, flipped open to the last page.

Nurtic Ehud Leavesleft

To the Diving Commander ~~Cease Terminus Lechatelierite~~,

In accordance with the first law of legal blockading, the South Conflagrablaze Captive has formally declared a siege against the North Ichthyosis Island and the Democratic-Republic of Nuria, as of January 8th of the 94th age (7th Era). The Second Earth Order investigated the claims made by the Conflagrian System and has consequently become aware of the illegal 'Second War Pact of the 92nd Age.' The Free Peoples of Oriya, the Order Authority, sent an ultimatum to the Nurian government requesting Nuria either breach the Alliance immediately or suffer expulsion from the Second Earth Order. Nuria has therefore decided to terminate the Nurro-Ichthyothian Alliance and withdraw its manpower from all Ichthyothian Military bases by January 8, 94. Your cooperation is anticipated and appreciated.

Respectfully,

Nurian President Georgen Winster Briggesh

I looked up at Leavesleft, jaw unhinged. In seconds, our whole world turned upside-down.

"I'm sorry, sir," I mumbled stupidly.

"Why?" Leavesleft asked very quietly, in Nurian. He usually made a special effort to speak Ichthyothian to us base-raised.

I blinked. "What?"

"Why are you sorry?" I was unused to hearing Leavesleft's voice so somber. So hard.

What kind of question was that? "You have to forfeit command and leave Icicle," I answered, shifting to Nurian myself. "You and all your countrymen have to give up the fight and go home."

Leavesleft didn't blink, face free of its usual smile-dimples. "Isn't that what you want? Won't all you Ichthyothians be glad to see us *rookies* go?" It struck a chord to hear him use the demeaning word we often called them. It was the only Ichthyothian word in his sentence. "Nuria didn't have any enemies until Ichthyosis introduced us to this war. Before you, Nuria didn't even know how to fight." He took the report from my sweaty hands. "You brilliant Ichthyothians have more respect for the ruthless System than you do for the brothers who fight and die at your sides." His quiet words hit me harder than Cease's loud reprimands ever did. "But, Ichthyosis is free of its deadweight, now."

With that, Leavesleft reached for his left sleeve and tore off the three rank bands. They came off easily, as though halfheartedly stitched on, in the first place. As if Leavesleft somehow knew when he was promoted that this day was around the corner. The day the alliance fell.

He stood, called the fleet to attention and stoically delivered the news, first in his language, then in mine, though no one really needed the Ichthyothian translation. The Nurians gaped openly. The Ichthyothians sat stone still.

But, I could see something subtle in their pale eyes, undermining their apparent nonchalance.

It was fear. Fear of being abandoned in this critical stage of the war. Fear of losing our only lifeline in this cold, isolated world. The lifeline we never respected.

"The alliance stands until a minute before midnight, on January seventh," Leavesleft continued. "Until then, we are still the Nurro-Ichthyothian Diving Fleet. If we're called into battle within these next couple days, it's our responsibility—Nurians and Ichthyothians alike—to give it everything we've got." Leavesleft's soft voice captured everyone's undivided attention for the first time during his brief commandership. "Ichthyosis, you're not alone, yet. Until the eighth, my people are still here, standing beside you."

Leavesleft gave his post his all. I had to admit, he really tried. With only sixteen months under his belt, he did everything he could to walk in the boots of a man with eighteen ages of experience. Of course, I shouldn't have expected as much from the Nurians—who grew up in the distracting world of public schools, fast food, recess breaks and reality television—as I did from us base-raised soldiers, set on a single track since birth: to kill and destroy.

And, without Nuria, there would only be twenty-seven divers left at Icicle Base.

PART II
THE SEVENTH

"[They] revealed their military training in the way they walked, in the set of their shoulders...

in the way their eyes watched and watched and watched."

—Dune *by Frank Herbert*

AMBREK COPPERTUS

January seventh, two o'clock.

I crept across the coarse sand, still warm from the day's sun, hand poised on the hilt of my sword. I could see the Fire Pit flicker in the near-distance, sending weak wisps of smoke into the dusty, brown, night sky. These pathetic, magicless flames were a gift from the Ichthyothians. The faint, scarlet-red Pit seemed to cry out for the crystal shard that now lay in the frigid Septentrion Sea, thousands of miles away.

I knocked on the splintered, auburn door of Seventh Cabin, tapping a particular rhythm with my knuckles to let those inside know it was a friend. It creaked open.

"Coppertus?" Prunus Persica stared at me in surprise. Great. I didn't expect Fair's quasi-boyfriend to be the one guarding the incendiary tonight, since he did it last night. At some point in the last five months, I must've aroused his suspicions or rubbed him the wrong way, because he—and his grandfather, Ivan 'Ivy' Leaf, a willowy, old man named for the color green—always seemed on-guard around me. The Red Revolution attracted a lot of insurgent-types who were easily riled up and didn't think for themselves, but Persica wasn't one of them. He was one of the sharper arrows in Scarlet's quiver. I considered him somewhat of a threat to my cover.

"Today's the day," I said in my most confident tone. "Scarlet and I are going to attack the Mage Castle. I need *it*."

While all the Reds besides Fair and Scarlet were as ignorant as ever of our plot to retrieve the fragment, they were aware we intended to infiltrate a sea battle for the purpose of getting our hands on a ship and deploying a bomb.

Persica gave me a long, hard look before letting me in and leading me to where the finished product was stashed. He lifted the tiny, two-pound, aluminum and magnesium incendiary from a stone box and handed it to me, carefully, as though it were a fragile dragon egg. I tucked it into the folds of my robe and gave him a curt nod of thanks.

I turned to go, only to find Ivy Leaf standing in the doorway. Wonderful.

"Where is the Red One? And, Gabardine?" He looked down his long, crooked nose, hazel-green eyes narrowed.

"Headquarters," I answered.

"You came here all by yourself, in the middle of the night?" He folded his spindly arms.

"Well, it seemed more discreet than broad daylight."

"This is a dangerous region—much more so than where Headquarters is. We're too close to the Mage Castle. You shouldn't have come here alone."

I was getting impatient. Anapes was expecting me.

"Scarlet thought an entourage would be a little conspicuous," I said, testily. "Now, I've got to go. Got a few things to take care of before the battle."

And, before Leaf could prod further, I pushed past him and ducked into the night.

I told Scarlet I set off early to oversee the final developments of the incendiary, asking them to meet me in front of Seventh Cabin this evening, an hour before the System Water Forces deployed.

"You're late," Anapes greeted me crossly, upon my arrival at the Mage Castle.

"Sorry, sir," I muttered, wiping my bloody palm on the inside of my pocket. Still accustomed to hand spectrum—lifelong habits died hard, I supposed—I didn't think twice before pushing aside a thorny plant with my bare hands, on my way through the woods. Any obvious injuries, I'd have to explain to Scarlet later. "Persica and his grandfather were giving me trouble." As usual.

Anapes wasn't listening. "Do you have it?"

Wordlessly, I pulled the thin, light cylinder from my robe and handed it to him.

"This?" he breathed, eyes wide. "*This* can take down a Nordic skyscraper?"

"Don't judge its might by its size," I answered, knowing all too well that sometimes, the smallest things could wreak the most havoc; just look at Scarlet and Lechatelierite, who probably didn't break two-hundred pounds, put together.

While I changed into my flightsuit, Anapes installed the firebomb in the little plane I was going to take. I was posing as a private delivery from Ichthyosis. Which meant I had to look like I was coming from Ichthyosis. Which meant I had to overshoot, a lot—across the Briny Ocean and partway across the Septentrion Sea—then double back. And, while overshooting, I couldn't fly too close to any Nordic military facilities, lest I come within eyeshot (thankfully, until this day, the Nordics' radars still didn't function properly, thanks to the serious damage the System inflicted back in the summer). Only after this great loop could I come home.

In total, I would fly about five-thousand miles.

"Are you sure the plane carries enough fuel for all this?" I asked Anapes.

"Yes," he responded, irritably. "Now, hurry up; I want you back for the battle tonight. If, for any reason, you don't think you'll be able to make it in time, just let me know."

I'd be letting him know, that was for sure. But, he was in the dark about that. He hadn't a clue that I did, in fact, plan on deploying this evening with the Water Forces, just not as myself. And, with Scarlet. No one in the System could know about our plan to retrieve the crystal fragment. The credit of the spectral recrystallization had to be mine alone.

It was going to be the longest day of my life. I was a nervous wreck, not only because I had to bomb a skyscraper this morning, but also infiltrate my own army tonight. As I took off, I tried to comfort myself by going over all the reasons the clandestine mission would likely be a success. Firstly, Cu Twentnine and Rusty Pypes weren't exactly the finest hatches in the dragon's nest—they were no match for Scarlet and I. Secondly, when it came to finding the crystal, I had the best possible guide-dragon—Scarlet's sense of awareness was truly remarkable, even without magic. And, as we got closer to the fragment, Scarlet's eye-spectrum would return, enabling her to spot it in no time. Thirdly, the Nordic Fleet was primarily manned by bumbling Nurians, which increased our chances of slipping away unnoticed and unscathed. And, lastly, the Diving Fleet was without Lechatelierite, the enemy soldier most likely to figure out what we were up to and hunt us down. Whoever was installed in his place—Scarlet anticipated it'd be Inexor Buird, the POW who escaped the day my sister died—may be good, but still no Lechatelierite.

The flight dragged on. By the time I U-turned, my overactive imagination began conjuring up vivid images of the Nurian Trade Centerscraper in flames. Thirty minutes outside of Alcove City, I was sick to my stomach. Literally. I doubled over in the cockpit, hyperventilating, on the brink of retching into my helmet. The Centerscraper was hundreds of stories tall. I swallowed. Thousands of people worked there. My hands grew sweaty beneath my olive-green gloves. Thousands of…civilians. The Briny Ocean rushed beneath my wings. Anapes said this was 'total war.' The entire enemy community was a valid object of war. And, I told him I was okay with that.

But, maybe, I wasn't. It was one thing for soldiers to die in the line of fire—to enlist in the military was to willingly consider your life expendable for your nation. Civilians, however, made no such vow. The people in the Nurian Trade Centerscraper certainly didn't. These men and women simply woke up in the morning and headed off to work as usual, to support their families and livelihoods.

This wasn't war. This was murder.

I was worse than Lechatelierite.

The thought filled me with dread and fear. I entered the city. My hands shook on the console as I looked down at the endless expanse of silver-blue skyscrapers. Civilians. And, they weren't even Ichthyothian. I was used to thinking of only Ichthyosis as the System's enemy in the international war. I hated Ichthyothians—maybe, I'd feel better if I were about to bomb an Ichthyothian facility. But, this was Nuria. Nuria was simply stuck in the middle of our war. Literally, sandwiched. This country only joined the fight because of Lechatelierite's malicious trickery.

And, the Nurians I was about to kill now were civilians.

I spotted the Centerscraper among the countless buildings crowding the skyline. It was the tallest structure for miles.

'7:19.'

Civilians.

I began punching in the unlocking code for the bomb bay.

'7:20.'

Innocent people.

I peered down and saw the Centerscraper's adjoining factories, puffing black smoke into the pale, early-morning sky.
'7:21.'
Murder.
A string of hot-off-the-assembly-line, commercial fishing vessels were parked by the southern wing of one of the factories. At the northern wing, basking in the crisp dawn light, were two rows of newly-minted, Ichthyothian crystalline shuttles.
'7:22.'
Ichthyothian crystallines.
My chest tightened as I stared at the sleek, enemy warships, fins emblazoned with that hateful, cobalt-blue, triangle logo. There were dozens of them.
'7:23.'
In the light, they were silver-grey. The color of the eyes that haunted my nightmares, since the summer. The color of the eyes that looked down at my sister's dead body without a shadow of remorse. The color of the eyes that stole the heart and loyalties of my betrothed.
Nuria wasn't innocent. Nuria committed itself to supporting Ichthyosis, not just with food and textiles, but wartime aid. Ships and weapons and soldiers. Thousands of soldiers. Nuria helped Ichthyosis steal our spectrum—Conflagria's only lifeline in this isolated world, the one asset that set our nation apart and gave us a chance to rise above obscurity on Second Earth, joining the ranks of the mighty, technological powers. Nuria was just another arrogant, Nordic overlord who believed miracle-making—whether by tech or by magic—should be reserved for themselves, denied of us.
'7:24.'
I circled the Centerscraper, finger hovering over the bomb-release button. Now, now! I screamed in my mind.
'7:25.'

The tiny, two-pound bundle of destruction dropped from my shaft. Its toter flew open, spraying the roof with kindles and canisters of napalm; they twirled in the air like glittering snow-crystals. Upon contact, the white flakes turned to little, scarlet-red flames that flickered for a few seconds like naïve candles before erupting into enormous, blue-white conflagrations. Chunks of metal melted off the building and avalanched onto the bustling streets below like a flaming meteor shower, igniting passing flivvers, the rows of vessels, and the adjoining factories. When one particular factory caught fire, it exploded as though it were a bomb itself—I wondered why that was. I peeled out, flames licking my tail. Night-black columns of smoke and amber-gold heatwaves twisted into the sky, thicker than those that once rose from the Fire Pit back when it was still brimming with spectrum.

And, it was Scarlet's genius that made all this possible.

I wrenched my eyes from the terrifying sight and shot off into the distance, back home to Conflagria. As I rode in silence, I felt something inside me die.

FINIS LECHATELIERITE

I gazed out the grand window behind my desk, down at the busy streets of Alcove City, the capital of the nation that no longer stood with my homeland in the war. The alliance my son forged only sixteen months ago fell apart. And, the impending sea blockade was going to wreck my company, tank the Nurian economy, literally starve out Ichthyosis, and capsize the Resistance.

I wondered if Scarlet July had anything to do with the security leak.

Despite the alliance's collapse, my business would finish the 'Cobalt-60 Project'—it was grandfathered in. Our customer was the Trilateral Committee. They commissioned it about five months ago, shortly after the Crystal's end, and it was both classified and controversial. Even my son and the Diving Fleet were completely in the dark about it. The TC had been keeping it from Cease because he was what they called a 'mage sympathizer.' The TC would order the Air Force to administer the finished product. Cease would only find out when it was too late.

Second Earth was void of uranium and plutonium and anything that could be used for nuclear warfare. But, recently, a few of my chemists discovered neutron activation could concoct a synthetic isotope called 'cobalt-60' which could be used to create a 'dirty bomb'—a fusion of radioactive material and conventional explosives. A dirty bomb was certainly no nuclear weapon, but it was the next best thing. While the doctored isotope wouldn't add force to the blastwave—it'd still have the destructive radius of whatever regular explosive it was mixed with—it'd make the fallout radioactive. Yesterday, my company succeeded in producing Second Earth's very first dirty bomb—it was currently in a safe in one of the Centerscraper's adjoining factories, the Krustallos Finire VI Wing. The Air Force would drop it in the Conflagrian Fire Pit by the end of next week. Conflagria was tiny, so it was estimated that at least a third of the island's total population—Reds and System supporters alike—would be exposed to some degree of poisonous radiation. The Trilateral Committee decided it didn't care for the Red Revolution. And, neither did I. Reds, System supporters—they were all the same to me. Conflagrians were Conflagrians; they were a menace to Second Earth and humanity was better off without them.

The strange rumble suddenly sounded, as though a dozen snow-blowers simultaneously whirred to life right inside my office. Where was the noise coming from? And, why was it getting so hot in here?

A giant, fiery chunk of metal came tumbling from the sky out of nowhere, whipping past my window like a flaming meteor. It crashed spectacularly into the roof of the Krustallos Finire VI Wing. No. No! The factory exploded before my very eyes, pelting my window with radioactive debris. Ears ringing from the deafening bang, I cowered under my desk, gasping, coughing and crying, as thick, black smoke seeped into my office from the crack below my closed door, collecting at the ceiling like storm-clouds. In seconds, the smog satiated the entire room.

Thank God that Qui was out getting breakfast, now. But, I knew, she'd still be affected by the dirty bomb's radiation, no matter where she was in the city.

I felt as though my very bones were on fire. Sweat trickled down my body like caustic venom. It was unbearable. I needed relief. Now. I hurled myself out my window. I tumbled through the air as though diving from a vitreous silica, the city street rushing up at me—

The water pressure was intense! Every muscle in my body fought incredible resistance. And, it was far colder than the coldest winter I'd experienced yet. Tiny shards of ice pressed into my skintight, white suit. I held onto the sides of a metal sub, racing through the frigid sea. Where was I? How did I get here? Fighting panic, I peered up through my helmet's visor, toward the surface. My stomach knotted when I saw how far it was. There was no escape. My fingers ached from holding the handlebars so tightly. Cobalt blue stretched endlessly in every direction… except one. There was a small light ahead. It flickered and twisted. No. It couldn't possibly be what I thought it was, because I was underwater.

Let go! someone silently screamed, but my body refused to obey. *Let go, or you'll die!* Finally, my white-gloved hands uncurled. With the blink of an eye, fire engulfed the sub. I tumbled wildly into the current—

It was Scarlet's voice! But, inside Cease's head. I was catching a glimpse of the battle Cease lost! This was it. This was how Scarlet saved him.

How was I seeing this? Was I having a…vision? An Ichthyothian, having a vision? If *that* was possible, maybe Cease wasn't insane after all, but actually—

CEASE LECHATELIERITE

"The court-martial of the Nurro-Ichthyothian Diving Commander Cease Terminus Lechatelierite is hereby commencing as of seven o'clock on this seventh day of January of the ninety-fourth age of the seventh era," the voice of the Ichthyothian-born Judge, Dne Latsyrc, sounded from the great, wooden podium. "The defendant's charges are as follows: authorizing the military service of a Conflagrian mage in the Nurro-Ichthyothian Diving Fleet from May twenty-fourth of the ninety-third age to August seventh of the ninety-third age; disregarding executive surrender orders by commanding an offensive against the System Water Forces Base in the Fervor Sea on July twenty-fifth of the ninety-third age; and subjecting Conflagrian Prisoner-of-War Fair Antiquartz Gabardine to inhumane treatment as defined by the Geneva Convention, on July twenty-sixth of the ninety-third age. Witnesses against the accused are as follows: Diving Fleet Colonel Autoero Augustus Austere, Diving Fleet Unit Three Officer Illia Eci Frappe, and Icicle Base Nurse Insouci Rorret Raef." The judge paused to glare at me. "You are Diving Commander Cease Terminus Lechatelierite, correct?"

I stood with my hands at my sides, fists balled, breathing in the stifling-hot air of the Alcove City Military Courthouse. Lawyering was abolished on Second Earth, having caused a lot of trouble and inefficiency on First Earth. So, I was representing myself today. And, as always, I was happy to fight my own battles.

"Yes…Your Honor," I answered stiffly.

"Did you not permit Scarlet Carmine July, a native of the enemy state of the South Conflagrablaze Captive, to enlist and serve in the Nurro-Ichthyothian Diving Fleet from May twenty-fourth of the ninety-third age to August seventh of that same age?"

Enemy state? I could feel my fuse shorten, already. "I did, but–"

"Did you not authorize her service without consulting or notifying the Trilateral Committee, though fully aware that the Second War Pact of the Ninety-Second Age specifies only Nurian and Ichthyothian citizens are permitted to join the Nurro-Ichthyothian military?" he pressed.

"I did, but—"

"Were you not the one who authored the Pact, including the provision outlining all terms and conditions of service?"

"Yes, but—"

"The court calls Colonel Autoero Augustus Austere to the stand."

Austere rose from his seat and marched to the plinth, a red folder clutched in his hands, blue eyes set.

"Colonel, were you or any other Nurro-Ichthyothian military personnel aware of Scarlet Carmine July's nationality at the time of her admission into the Nurian Diving Academy on October seventh of the ninety-second age?"

"No, Your Honor," Austere responded. "Upon beginning the admissions process for the academy, Scarlet July provided false documentation indicating she was from Alcove City, Nuria, a graduate of Bay River Secondary School."

"Were you or any other Nurro-Ichthyothian military personnel aside from the defendant aware of Scarlet Carmine July's nationality at the time of her acceptance into the Nurro-Ichthyothian Diving Fleet on May twenty-fourth of the ninety-third age?"

"No, Your Honor. Upon meeting her that day, the Commander immediately grew suspicious of her origins and subjected her to interrogation." He pulled a document from his folder. "I have here a copy of the report the Commander composed thereafter." An attendant walked over to Austere, took the packet from him and carried it to Judge Latsyrc's podium. "On page two, Commander Lechatelierite states that, and I quote, 'though Scarlet July is a Conflagrian mage, she is completely trustworthy and would be an invaluable asset to the fleet,'" Austere declared, and I felt a rush of gratitude toward him.

"The content of the report is irrelevant, Colonel," the judge said.

"It is NOT!" I burst.

"Order!" He banged his gavel. "Commander Lechatelierite, you are not permitted to speak while a witness is on the stand!" He turned back to Austere. "The concern here is Miss July's nationality, Colonel, not her so-called 'trustworthiness.'"

"Yes, Your Honor," Austere resigned.

Anger welled in my chest as I remembered my latest vision of Scarlet. I guessed I was wrong about her, after all. A part of me still couldn't believe it. I thought I had her figured out. I thought she was someone I could trust with both my country and my heart. What could've possibly happened since the summer to make her turn her back on everything she fought for? To make her turn her back on me?

Whenever I replayed August seventh in my head, I noticed something. When I told her I loved her, she stayed quiet. I always assumed she was just too surprised or nervous to speak. I thought there was no way she could kiss me so passionately and not love me back. But, now, I knew better. If she ever loved who I was and what I stood for, she wouldn't dream of selling out to the System, mere months later.

Judge Latsyrc clasped his hands together and leaned forward. "Colonel, when did Commander Lechatelierite make the content of that report available for review by other military personnel?"

"Not until July twenty-sixth of the ninety-third age, Your Honor. Prior to then, he kept the file encrypted and password-protected."

"What information regarding the interrogation did the Commander verbally relay to his comrades on the morning of May twenty-fifth of the ninety-third age?"

"He stated his suspicions were wrong and that Scarlet July isn't Conflagrian, but Nurian."

"So, he blatantly lied, without just cause, to the entire fleet?"

"Objection!" I called. "I did have 'just cause'; I had no choice but to conceal her origins for the time being, to prevent intra-army conflict during a volatile time of internal transition, not to mention a critical state of the war—"

"Silence!" Latsyrc flared. "You are not to talk out of turn again, Commander Lechatelierite!" He looked back at Austere. "Thank you, Colonel. You may return to your seat."

"Thank you, Your Honor."

"Commander Lechatelierite, *now* do you wish to comment on the issue of just cause?"

"Yes, I certainly would, Your Honor," I said, standing. "I didn't take my decision to let Scarlet July serve lightly, and I didn't hide her heritage from my men on a whim. In deciding to conceal the intel for a brief period, I was strategically and actively preserving the community of trust and comradery upon which the fleet's operation depended, both protecting Scarlet July's wellbeing and safeguarding the emotional stability of my base-raised subordinates who were already facing the tough task of adapting to and learning to trust seventy new recruits from a radically different, civilian culture. The Childhood Program—and, to an extent, the Nurian Diving Academy, too—teaches its students to hate all things magical. The academies don't differentiate between the System—our true enemy—and the innocent Conflagrian civilians. Keeping Scarlet's secret until the time was right was the only safe and sensible option I had, for all parties involved.

"Moreover, by authorizing Scarlet's service, I was defending the best interests of the alliance and, I daresay, the future of the northwestern hemisphere. If Second Commander Scarlet Carmine July never wore the white and blue of the Nurro-Ichthyothian Military, the Core Crystal—the instrument by which the System maintained its absolute control over the Conflagrian masses—would still be in existence today and, therefore, the spectral web would've never diffused."

Murmurs broke out across the courthouse as Latsyrc's grey-speckled eyebrows shot to the rim of his receding hairline. "Are you claiming Miss July is responsible for the destruction of the magical powersource?"

"Yes, Your Honor," my voice sliced into the hubbub. "And, she was quite literally the only person on Second Earth who could do it."

"Impossible!" Latsyrc roared. "Mages were subject to the System's spectral thought-suppression. There's no way any Conflagrian could've committed such an act of defiance. The glaringly obvious motive for her service in your fleet was that she was a double-agent, an enemy infiltrator!"

"You're wrong, Your Honor. Scarlet July was the Multi-Source Enchant; she harnessed enough of the Crystal's energy to be immune to the System's spectral dominion.

She was therefore capable of independent thought, choosing to serve the alliance with loyalty and honor." At times like these, I was especially grateful for my exceptional vocal control because, as far as I was concerned, Scarlet July was as loyal and honorable as Principal Tincture.

The hum in the room grew so loud, the judge had to pound his gavel to get everyone to shut up.

"But, the concept of the 'Multi-Source Enchant' is just Conflagrian folklore," he breathed. "A myth!"

"I have evidence of Scarlet's extraordinary spectral status." I pulled my visual band from under my collar, snapped it across my eyes, pulled a few pages from my binder and passed them to the attendant, who handed them to the judge. "After her interrogation, I requested she undergo a series of spectral diagnostics usually given to our Conflagrian POWs. These tests confirmed she had two power-sources—eyes and hair—and that her Blood Spectrum Content, or BSC, was several points higher than the average, adult mage. She was the Conflagrian Multi-Source Enchant. Her exceptional dominion over the spectral web both enabled her to act on her own free will and physically enabled her to end the Crystal. On July thirty-first of the ninety-third age, she reached into the Conflagrian Fire Pit with her hair and literally crushed the Crystal, diffusing the entire spectral network. No other weapon—magical or non—could've done that. And, no other mage mind could've opposed the thought-suppression long enough to take such drastic and extensive action against the System."

Latsyrc paged through Scarlet's medical records for what felt like eras. Then, he lifted his head and faintly said, "The court will be checking on the validity of these documents within the hour."

I didn't blink. "Please do."

He passed the records back to the attendant, eyes still locked on mine. "Miss July may have become an asset to the alliance by the end of July. However, you couldn't have possibly known of her ability to destroy the Core Crystal—which you are now seeking to use as justification for breaking mandate seventeen of the Second War Pact—at the actual time you accepted her into your fleet on May twenty-fourth. Her unique talents only happened to come in handy, two full months after you made that call. You weren't even aware of the existence of the Core Crystal until the interrogation of Conflagrian POW Fair Antiquartz Gabardine on July twenty-sixth, correct?"

I dug my nails into my palms. "Your Honor, Scarlet's usefulness to the Nurro-Ichthyothian Resistance was neither a coincidence nor a surprise to me. Of course, I couldn't have known back in May exactly how it'd play out in the months to come. But, from the start, I intended to exploit her special spectral gifts and inside knowledge of magekind for the benefit of the alliance. That's the reason I decided not only to keep her in my fleet but to promote her to second-in-command: I knew she could offer me what no one else could. And, indeed, the alliance reaped an invaluable benefit from Scarlet's service: the diffusion. No one can deny the importance of the diffusion."

Latsyrc scoffed, "None of this changes the fact you defied mandate seventeen of the Second War Pact of the Ninety-Second Age, which specifies that only those from the allied nations are permitted to serve in the Nurro-Ichthyothian military."

I was silent.

The judge made a sweeping gesture with his hand. "Ladies and gentlemen of the jury, the author of the Pact himself!" He glared at me. "You're not above the law, Commander Lechatelierite. 'Leader of the Resistance' or not, you cannot just do whatever you like without the approval of *your* superiors, the Trilateral Committee. You do not have the authority to trust a Conflagrian citizen with the fate of your people."

The room was quiet.

"She was no longer a Conflagrian citizen," I suddenly said.

"Excuse me?"

"Your Honor, at the time of her enlistment," I swallowed, "Scarlet July was no longer a Conflagrian citizen. She was deported to Nuria on July twenty-fifth of the eighty-seventh age. It was exile. She lived for five ages as a civilian Nurian, working as a conductor for the Alcove City train station."

"There's no way to verify the claims you're making, regarding her exile. We can't exactly call the System to the stand, now can we?"

"But, you can ask her previous employers about her work there. Before her military service, Scarlet spent five solid ages as a productive member of Nurian society. Contact the train station."

Latsyrc furrowed his bushy, salt-and-pepper eyebrows, scribbled on his legal pad and mumbled something to the attendant, who scurried off, presumably to make the call.

"The court will now proceed to addressing the defendant's second charge: disobeying a direct order from the Nurian and Ichthyothian heads-of-state to surrender to the South Conflagrablaze Captive, choosing instead to immediately initiate an offensive against the System Water Forces Fervor Sea Base. Commander Lechatelierite, on the morning of July twenty-fifth of the ninety-third age, did you not receive a letter addressed directly to you, signed by Ichthyothian Prime Minister Rime Gelid Ascet, Nurian President Georgen Winster Briggesh and Alliance Chairman Cartel Aliquot Juncture, requesting your immediate surrender to the South Conflagrablaze Captive on behalf of the Nurro-Ichthyothian Alliance?"

"I did, but—"

"And, did you not blatantly disregard that command by ordering your fleet to attack the System Water Forces Base in the Fervor Sea, later that same day?"

"I did, but—"

"There is no 'but' here, Commander. There's nothing to explain away. You were clearly instructed to surrender and you disobeyed." He turned to the bench. "The court calls Nurro-Ichthyothian Diving Fleet Unit Three Officer Illia Eci Frappe to the stand."

Illia rose from his seat and marched to the plinth, brown eyes vacant.

"Officer Frappe, were you not with the Commander on the morning of July twenty-fifth of the ninety-third age, when he received the state-of-the-war report containing the executive order to surrender?"

"I was, Your Honor," he responded, mechanically.

"Did the Commander share the content of the letter with you or anyone in the fleet before dispatch?"

"No, Your Honor."

"How and when did you learn about the surrender order?"

"The following morning, Second Commander Scarlet July stood up in front of everyone in the mess hall and read it out loud."

Did she now? When I kamikazed into the Fervor Sea Base, I was sure I was leaving my fleet in the hands of someone who'd continue the fight, no matter what. Someone who'd never stand down. Someone who'd continue my legacy, against all odds. I always trusted Scarlet whole-heartedly, with everything. She had me completely under her spell, all along.

"On the morning of July twenty-fifth of the ninety-third age, before deploying, the Commander did not reveal the content of the report with any of his men?"

"That's correct, Your Honor," Frappe answered, voice placid. "He sat in front of me at breakfast and read it silently, then immediately ordered us to deploy without disclosing a thing."

Latsyrc nodded. "Thank you, Officer Frappe. You may take your seat."

Shaking with silent rage, I spoke through gritted teeth. "Permission to speak, Your Honor?" It felt strange, to ask someone that. I wasn't used to asking permission of others, for anything. I was always the one in charge.

He gave an exasperated sigh, as is if it were totally outrageous for the defendant to speak at his own trial. "Proceed."

I stood. "According to the eighty-seventh mandate of the Second War Pact, the decision to surrender must be made unanimously by the Alliance Committee, Trilateral Committee and the executive offices of both states, correct?"

The judge nodded, fanning a copy of the surrender order before the courtroom. "I do indeed see the signatures of the Nurian and Ichthyothian heads-of-state and the Alliance Committee and Trilateral Committee Chairmen on this document."

"How strange," I interjected obnoxiously, putting my hand to my chin, "because I don't recall participating in any sort of vote, last summer."

"Watch your tone, Commander!"

"Permission to speak, Your Honor," a throaty voice issued from the far, right corner of the room. I turned and saw none other than Admiral Oppre Sive, the chief of the Trilateral Committee, in full ceremonial uniform, shirt prim and pressed, chest covered in pins and medals. I myself had a Silver Triangle—the highest honor a diver could receive—but, of course, it was back home in my Icicle quarters, out-of-reach. I wondered what Judge Latsyrc would think if he knew the Trilateral Committee awarded me a Silver Triangle in August, knowing full well I'd just attacked the Fervor Sea Base, tortured Fair Gabardine and had my Conflagrian second-in-command destroy the Core Crystal.

"Permission granted."

The Admiral strode to the front of the courtroom. "Commander Lechatelierite," he said, "at the time, you were in battle, almost daily. It was simply impossible to pull you away from Icicle for this conference."

"Then, it should've been postponed!"

"That wasn't an option, either," he responded, coolly. "Those were desperate times; the meeting was held on an emergency basis. Besides, such a decision wouldn't require the input from a lowly commander."

Lowly commander? I could almost feel vapor issue from my ears. The sentiment of a pack of detached, out-of-touch, retired admirals and commodores carried more weight than that of a foot-soldier who came face-to-face with the enemy almost every day?

"And, according to the official registry," he continued, "at the time, you were not a member of the Alliance Committee."

Not a member? "How's that possible? I wrote the treaty that *created* the alliance! I'm the *Leader of the Nurro-Ichthyothian Resistance!* How's any vote determining the war's outcome valid without my input?"

Once again, a buzz swept across the courtroom and Latsyrc banged his gavel.

"Order, order," he said, gruffly. "Thank you, Commander Lechatelierite. You've made your point. Please take your seat." A new attendant entered and handed Latsyrc a fat document. "We will now proceed to the defendant's third and final charge: the abuse of Conflagrian Prisoner-of-War Fair Antiquartz Gabardine on July twenty-sixth of the ninety-third age." Latsyrc flipped a few pages. "The Trilateral Committee mandates that prisoners-of-war be treated humanely, in accordance with the First Earth Geneva Convention of '1906 BC,' which requires that, and I quote, 'a prisoner-of-war shall not be dealt with by his or her captors as a criminal, but may be employed in paid, nonmilitary work. The prisoner bears the right to obtain adequate food, clothing, quarters and the transmission of letters and parcels. An enemy soldier is bound to reveal his or her name, rank and serial number, but cannot legally be compelled to give further information to his or her captors.'

"Fair Antiquartz Gabardine, the former Leader of Flame Team Seven of the System Water Forces, was allegedly abused during an interrogation conducted by the defendant. There are no first-hand witnesses besides Scarlet Carmine July, who is presently unattainable for examination by the Nurro-Ichthyothian Military Court of Alcove City. However, testimony will be obtained from an Icicle Base medical professional who treated the prisoner following her interrogation. The court calls Mrs. Insouci Rorret Raef to the stand."

Nurse Raef walked to the plinth, dark-blue eyes wide and fearful, platinum-blonde hair pulled back in a sloppy bun. She passed a data drive to the attendant. Her wavering voice accompanied a series of grotesque images projected in rapid succession on the white wall before us.

"In addition to the physical trauma pictured here," she said, "Dr. Calibre and I believe Miss Gabardine also sustained severe psychological abuse." The nurse's watery eyes rested on the floor as she proceeded to describe Fair's screaming, crying, cutting and food-refusal in the days following her interrogation. Apparently, Fair behaved like that right up until the hour Leavesleft shipped her back to Conflagria with Scarlet on August seventh. As she spoke, Raef seemed genuinely disturbed.

And, she wasn't alone.

As I looked around the courtroom, not a single face wasn't stricken with some degree of shock, terror, anger or grief—even Sive and Illia looked a little uncomfortable.

There was something wrong with me.

I pushed my visual band up my nose, stared intently at the pictures and willed myself to feel something. My mind acknowledged the horror on the wall, but only on an intellectual level. Because I also knew I had no other choice than to do what I did. I tried to play nice with Fair, at first—merely raising my voice and repeating my questions over and over—but, that wasn't enough to make her talk. So, I was forced to push things further and further until she finally did. And, the intel I pulled from her was invaluable. Without it, the System would've won the war, by now. The spectral web would've never diffused. Ichthyosis would be imperialized. Torturing Fair was necessary. It was the only way.

I remembered the one thing that *did* seriously hurt me, when I was through with Fair: the deep disappointment and disenchantment in Scarlet's gaze. Prior to that day, Scarlet only ever regarded me with respect or admiration. And, whenever she stared at me with awe in those glassy green eyes, I felt empowered. I felt like I could conquer the world. But, the night after the interrogation, Scarlet could barely look at me. I knew I let her down. And, that was what cut me.

Because, I admired her, too. I admired her emotional capacity. I admired the way she could grieve for Apha Edenta, though she never really knew him. I admired the way she believed every life was precious, no matter who or what they were. I admired the way she always saw the best in everyone. The way she always forgave and offered second chances. Even to someone who'd harm her best friend, right in front of her.

And, yet, she sold out to the System. All along, those beautiful eyes told of nothing but deception.

The slideshow ended. The judge offered me the floor, but I declined comment. There was nothing I could say to defend myself. I knew they'd never see Fair's torture as a logical necessity. They wouldn't believe I didn't hurt Fair to live out some sick, twisted fantasy or for any stupid, emotional reason, at all. How could I explain that torturing her was what my duty required? That, without the intel, Ichthyosis wouldn't be free anymore? That the diffusion was worth it? No one would understand.

For a time, last summer, I did develop the emotional capacity to feel sorry for what I did to Fair. But, that transformation was reversed now, and the person who stirred my heart in the first place was dead, as far as I was concerned.

The jury took a recess to deliberate. I knew what was coming my way, afterward. All it took was one guilty verdict. It didn't matter if I argued my way out of the first two charges—conviction of the third was all they needed to send me right back to prison. And, I knew, the end of my service in the fleet would mean the end for Ichthyosis.

All too soon, the court reconvened.

"As of nine o'clock on this seventh day of the first month of the ninety-fourth age, in the case of *North Ichthyosis Island versus Diving Commander Cease Terminus Lechatelierite*, the court hereby finds the defendant innocent of the first and second charges."

I exhaled. The judge's words were greeted by scattered, unenthusiastic applause.

"However, on the count of violating the Geneva Convention with the inhumane treatment of Conflagrian Prisoner-of-War Fair Antiquartz Gabardine, the court finds the defendant guilty."

"Your Honor," I blurted desperately, and murmurs erupted all around me, "I have reason to believe the spectral web is recrystallizing. I know it sounds crazy, but please hear me out: there's something in the sea causing intermittent bursts of magic. I'm positive. I need to go out there with my men, find out what's going on and put a stop to it, right away, before the diffusion is reversed for good."

"Silence!" he bellowed. "What is this foolishness? You are not permitted to talk out-of-turn!"

"Your Honor, please," I cried, "the fate of my country—*our* country—depends on it. This is bigger than you or me or this courtroom. This is about stopping the System from retaking absolute control of Conflagria and ultimately gaining the strength to imperialize the northwest. I just need to go out to sea one more time and figure this out. Right after, I'll leave my post and serve whatever time I owe; you can see to it. Please, just let me do this first."

"That's enough!"

"I'm the best military mind the alliance has got. And, I'm the only Nordic with a distinct sensitivity to the spectral web. I have to do this. Stop me and Ichthyosis doesn't stand a chance!"

He banged his gavel. "ORDER IN THE COURT!"

All went silent.

"As I was saying," Latsyrc half-shouted, hands gripping the podium, "*Mr.* Cease Lechatelierite is hereby discharged from the Nurro-Ichthyothian Diving Fleet and sentenced to seven months of detainment in—"

"Objection!" a voice cried from the back of the courtroom.

Every head turned. Two men in white uniform stood in the doorway. One was tall and lanky with bright-hazel eyes, sandy hair and a cross around his neck. The other was shorter and bulkier, with deep-blue eyes and buzzed, brown hair.

Nurtic Leavesleft and Inexor Buird.

"What's the meaning of this?" Latsyrc yelled. "Enough disruptions! No one is permitted to interrupt the delivery of a verdict!"

"Your Honor, my name is Nurtic Leavesleft and I'm the Commander of the Diving Fleet and current Resistance Leader. I'm here because President Briggesh and Prime Minister Ascet declared a state-of-emergency for each Nuria and Ichthyosis," Leavesleft announced, striding forward and brandishing a document, Inexor at his heels. I noticed that, oddly, the rank bands were missing from Leavesleft's left sleeve.

"As of when, and for what purpose?" the judge demanded. I supposed a national state-of-emergency was the one thing that could, in fact, interrupt the delivery of a verdict.

"As of the moment the Conflagrian System firebombed the Nurian Trade Centerscraper, Your Honor."

Every gear in my mind jammed.

"Firebombed?" Latsyrc breathed.

"There's been a terrorist attack while this trial was in session," Leavesleft said, "at seven-twenty-five. The System dropped an incendiary on the Centerscraper, destroying it and all surrounding factories."

The Nurian Trade Centerscraper. Firebombed. I dropped my binder loudly on the table but no one seemed to notice. Didn't my parents work there? Weren't most of my fleet's crafts manufactured there? What were we going to do without sufficient warship production?

"The Second Earth Order knows about the alliance, now," Inexor said, and all eyes shifted from Leavesleft to him, "and they threatened blacklisting if Nuria doesn't break it. President Briggesh is making the public announcement later today." Inexor swallowed. "Nuria has chosen to comply with the Order's request."

My knees felt weak. I didn't know knees actually did that. Much less, if those knees were mine. I put my fists on the table to steady myself.

"The alliance stands until a minute before midnight," Leavesleft said, "and Nuria intends to stay and fight, until then."

"Admirable sentence," the judge said, faintly, "and we're all shocked and grieved to hear of this unfortunate turn of events. But…why exactly did you come here? There's nothing we can do for you."

"That's where you're wrong," Inexor said, rather loudly. "The Nurro-Ichthyothian Military demands the temporary release of Cease Lechatelierite from trial and detainment. We need him to resume his post as Commander of the Diving Fleet, during the emergency."

Leavesleft walked up to the podium, paying no mind to the guard who tried to get in his way. "Your Honor, here are the release papers, signed by Commander Rai Zephyr of the Air Force, Commander Glace Slue of the Ground Troops, and by me," Leavesleft said solemnly, "the Leader of the Nurro-Ichthyothian Resistance."

The judge took the document from Leavesleft, wide-eyed and wordless.

Leavesleft and Inexor, the Nurian and the Ichthyothian, stood there, side by side, a true united front. Leavesleft could've easily sat back and waited out the final hours of his nation's commitment, but instead, he was using the little time he had left to take serious action. He rallied the support of the Air Force and Ground Troops and traveled fifteen-hundred miles in the fastest ship the fleet owned, to bust me out, because he wanted to make sure Ichthyosis would be left in good hands after the alliance fell.

And, there stood Inexor, willingly serving as the second-in-line to a man whose race he loathed. He stood there for the Resistance and for me, the man who demoted him, spat on his eleven ages of friendship and hurt the woman he claimed to love. Because, despite all that, he still trusted me and wanted me back, fighting alongside him. Leading him. Taking his life and the lives of our people into my hands.

War was a force terrible enough to destroy and divide. But, it was also a force terrible enough to unite. To wake you up and shock the priorities back into you.

Judge Dne Latsyrc may have been an insufferable fool, but in the end, he was still an Ichthyothian, above all, because then he said, "Very well. Commander Lechatelierite is free to go—for now. This session is adjourned."

Leavesleft and Inexor ran to me.

"Sir, we have intel that the System plans to approach the southwestern shore of Ichthyosis by nightfall," Leavesleft breathed. "We need you to command the defensive."

"My pleasure," I replied.

"Sir, everything you said about the spectral web re-crystallizing," he swallowed, "we believe. You need to find whatever's causing it, tonight, before the System does."

"I will," I said, "if it's the last thing I do."

"Cease," Inexor touched my shoulder, "it's good to have you back."

I nodded, following them out the door. And, for the first time since the diffusion, I actually felt proud to lead a fleet of both Ichthyothians and Nurians.

SCARLET JULY

As evening began to fall, Fair and I rode on scabrousback to Seventh Cabin to meet up with Ambrek. Smaller than pine dragons and much smaller and more docile than hobnails, scabrouses were a common mode of transportation on the island. While they couldn't fly like other breeds, they were strong enough to carry people and tow wagons. I would've preferred walking to the Castle through the forest to avoid attracting attention, but that would've taken way too long, plus we needed a means for Fair to transport the unconscious forms of Rusty Pypes and Cu Twentnine to Seventh after Ambrek and I deployed. Fair brought two extra robes with her, and a tarp to cover her rather unusual cargo.

When Fair and I arrived at Seventh, we found Ambrek already waiting for us outside, hair and robe rumpled, eyes wild.

"Ambrek," I squeaked, jumping off the scabrous and landing catlike in the sand, "are you okay?"

He blinked. "Yeah. Why wouldn't I be?"

"I don't know. You look…" I couldn't quite put my finger on it. There was something different about him. Something off. He seemed shaken up. On edge. And, also, on his guard. I frowned; this wasn't a good time for him to get into a funk. I needed him on his A-game. Conflagria's future literally depended on it. "You look…intense."

He smiled, but only with his lips. "It's been a rough day."

"How so?"

"I…got us a bit of a head-start. Already snuck in and out of the hangar to install our bomb into the shaft of fighter seven."

Wow. Already? By himself? How on Tincture's island did he manage that? "You're amazing, Ambrek," I breathed.

"Thanks; that means a lot, coming from you."

Fair rolled her eyes. "We interrupt this flirty flattery to warn you there's only an hour until dispatch. Come on!"

The three of us piled onto the scabrous. Ambrek was the driver, Fair was at the rear and I was squished in-between. Even without his hand magic, Ambrek maneuvered like a pro around the tree-trunks, bushes and low-hanging branches. I admired his dexterity and reflexes. I was sure he'd take to piloting well.

At some point, we halted, dismounted and tied the beast to a tree. With neither eye-spectrum nor a map, I hadn't a clue how Ambrek knew where in the forest to stop—this spot looked like any other. Ambrek dropped to his hands and knees and started pushing aside shrubbery and vines, unearthing a gate to a tunnel he claimed led directly to the Mage Castle's underground.

"How do you even know about this?" I asked him, yet again. Maybe this time I'd actually get an answer. Last night, when he first informed us of the tunnel's existence, he didn't explain a thing beyond, 'How else do you think Sixth Cabin and I completed our clandestine mission while you were away?' Even Fair was shocked to hear about it, and she used to be a flame team officer.

Ambrek looked at me with a mysterious glint in his gold eyes. "My sister built it," he whispered as we dropped through. Fair would follow soon. "She kept it a secret from the rest of the System."

That only raised more questions. "Why would the Commander of the Water Forces need a secret passage to her own base, much less tell her civilian brother about it?"

"Quiet while we're inside!" Ambrek hissed, suddenly stern and Cease-like. I pressed my lips together.

Deja-vu overcame me as I followed Ambrek down the winding staircase, descending into the darkness. Soon, we were confronted by a splitting path; I noticed a curious, orange-red flicker to our left.

"To the right," Ambrek instructed, rather tersely. He sure was being short with me. It was probably just nerves. After all, he'd only been a warrior for five months—this was the biggest mission of his life, thus far.

THUD!

"What was that?" I whispered, skidding to a stop.

"My head, hitting wood," he grunted. "I guess that means we're here." He shoved aside a floorboard and hoisted himself up. "Come on out."

But, I was too small to even reach the edge with my fingertips. So, Ambrek leaned into the opening, seized my ribcage and lifted me easily onto the landing. I felt so tiny and helpless in his grasp.

No, not helpless. Secure. Safe.

We were in a storage closet. An incredibly messy one. And, here I thought we Reds were the disorganized ones.

I noticed Ambrek left a bloody smudge on my robe. Alarmed, I grabbed his wrist. There was a deep cut, across his right palm.

I gasped. "Ambrek, how did you—"

He clamped his bleeding hand right over my mouth. "Shush!"

He was right; now was not the time. Though, I wasn't thrilled about Ambrek leaving his DNA everywhere. Not that the System had the means to conduct genetic tests without spectrum. I exhaled. I was just thinking like a Nordic, again.

Ambrek unceremoniously ushered me behind heap of dragonhide cases and no-longer-needed spectroscopy books. Crouching, he peered overhead. I was too short to see over the mess myself, even when standing upright. So, I had to peek between sloppily-stacked items.

"Rusty Pypes and Cu Twentnine should be here, any minute now," Ambrek whispered.

As if on cue, in came two men in dark-orange suits with olive-green helmets tucked under their arms. One of them had burnt-orange hair, and the other, golden-brown skin. They prowled around, gabbing loudly. As the carrot-top approached our hiding place, Ambrek balled his right fist.

"Hey Cu, take this!" Rusty called over his shoulder, reaching for a case.

At that moment, Ambrek jumped up and socked Rusty in the head. He dropped to the floor like a stone. Even without hand spectrum, Ambrek could throw a mean punch. I'd only ever seen Cease hit like that, and Cease spent his entire life learning to fight.

"Rusty?" Cu came rushing over. His eyes went wide when he spotted Ambrek. "Ambrek? What're you doing—"

Ambrek's fist collided with Cu's jaw. His limp body fell on top of Rusty's.

I gaped, "He knows your name?"

Ambrek looked alarmed for a moment, then shrugged. "Well, I *am* a Red co-leader. Is it really any surprise the enemy knows who the Multi-Source Enchant's right hand is?"

Good point.

We pulled off Rusty and Cu's clothes and dumped their half-naked bodies through the floorboard, where Fair would find them. Rusty was a runt of a man, but his suit was still several sizes too large. I nervously fumbled with all its confusing latches and fastenings. I didn't expect this baggy lump of cloth to really compare to the perfection of the evenly-heated, liquid-flexible, steel-strong, form-fitting, Ichthyothian diving suits.

From the corner of my eye, I saw Ambrek, fully dressed and ready to go.

"Whoa, you figured it out fast!"

He turned me around. "You crossed a couple latches. Let me get that for you."

How did he know? "The helmet is really weird, too. What do I do with this smaller part?" I held it up.

"That's the chin-guard. It's a separate compartment. Put on your helmet and I'll attach it for you."

Even the helmet was enormous. Nothing about this suit felt safe or secure. I wondered what my old comrades would think about going into the sea wearing *this*.

Ambrek plunked on Cu's helmet and said into the intercom, "Let's go!"

Hauling the case, we ran out into the hangar. I was appalled by the sheer size of the enemy army. Seven-hundred-plus System soldiers stood in block formation on the platform, facing a man at the front whom I assumed was the commander or captain. So, the System knew Ambrek's name, but I didn't even know who the leader of the Water Forces was.

"That's Captain Anapes Patrici," Ambrek's voice informed me. More intel from his unauthorized mission with Sixth Cabin?

"There you are, Pypes, Twentnine!" Patrici exclaimed as Ambrek and I scrambled into two of the three vacant spots in the seventh column. "You're late!"

"Sir," a soldier at the front of our line called. "My unit is down a man." He turned and looked back at us. "Where's Co–"

"He already alerted me he can't make it," Patrici cut across him. "He's still on his way back from Alcove City.

I don't know what the holdup is, but his mission was a success, so I'll cut him some slack."

What went on in Alcove City today? The theft of more ships?

"Alright, soldiers," Patrici said. "To your fighters. Dispatching, immediately!"

Stomach twisting, I followed Ambrek into our craft. I sat in the co-pilot seat and rapidly familiarized myself with the weapons panel I desperately hoped we wouldn't need. As I anticipated, the controls were just like that of the Ichthyothian scouts. What a relief. As Ambrek took off smoothly, I exhaled. It seemed he had a natural talent for pilotry.

All too soon, we reached the Septentrion Sea and were met by dozens of grey crystallines and hundreds of white suits.

The Nurro-Ichthyothian Diving Fleet.

The fleet I co-commanded, only five months ago.

The fleet in which many of my former comrades—whom I now thought of as old friends—probably still served, if they were lucky enough not to go the way of Apha Edenta, by now: Nurtic Leavesleft, Arrhyth Link, Dither Maine, Tose Acci. Oh Tincture, I even missed the likes of Illia Frappe and Quiesce Tacit, though I doubted the feeling was mutual.

But, I knew, Cease wasn't among them. The fleet was under someone else's command, now—Inexor, perhaps—because Ichthyosis willingly extinguished its brightest light.

Well, today, I had to force my heart to be grateful Cease wasn't here. Because, a mind like his stood the best chance of figuring out what Ambrek and I were up to, chasing us down and causing a stir. Likewise, I had to make myself thankful the fleet was underperforming as of late and was therefore less likely to intercept us. I had to put out of my mind what poor Cease must've been going through right now, kept away from his men when they needed him most, when everything was coming to a head. I had to try not to think about the alliance's bleak future without Cease's leadership…

Ambrek and I combed the reef, below which the brunt of the battle raged. Every so often, I glanced up at the chaos overhead. While individual soldier skill was clearly lacking amongst the Nordics, it appeared as though the fleet as a whole still operated with a sound strategy and a distinct sense of expertise and organization, as if Cease himself were the one in charge.

Ambrek and I gradually headed north, drawing ever nearer to the small peninsula known as Ichthyosis's seventh sector, where the tsunami carried vitreous silica debris from Cease's kamikaze-crash. Barely a mile from the shore now, I was yet to spot a thing or feel a photon of spectrum. I darted my magicless eyes back and forth across the expanse, contrasting every frosty ridge and bump to the image of the fragment I held in my no-longer-perfect memory. My hopes dulled with every passing second. I was starting to think we'd embarked on a wild scabrous chase.

And, then, just as my despair was about to peak, I saw it—the familiar, silvery, ovular stone I once carried in the pocket of my robe and wore around my neck. My breath caught in my chest.

"Ambrek, there it is! The crystal!"

Ambrek's helmeted head turned, wildly. "Where?"

"*Right there,* in front of us!" I jumped to my feet. "Quick, open the diving shaft!"

"Are you sure? I don't feel any magic."

My mind raced. "Well, its ideal environment is the Fire Pit, right? The Septentrion Sea is freezing—that's probably what's dampening its emissions."

"Totally snuffing out its emissions, you mean. It worked pretty well in the Briny Ocean."

"The Briny Ocean is a lot warmer than this. Now, come on, the double doors!"

BOOM!

Our display flashed: 'SHELDS: 87%.'

Ambrek faced the left window and muttered some nasty words I'd never heard him use before. I looked and saw a crystalline carrying a single surface-rider, whipping about in dizzying loops, like a horsefly. My heart thudded. I could recognize that intricate style of pilotry, any day. It was the trademark of Nurtic Leavesleft.

Nurtic's shuttle twirled as his surface-rider shot a hole through our right wing. Our shields dropped to seventy-seven percent.

"Scarlet, fire at them!" Ambrek's voice boomed in my helmet.

"What?" I blurted.

"Come on, they're going to take us out if you don't!"

I looked at the weapons panel and felt like vomiting. "I–I can't fire at Ichthyothians!"

"What choice do we have?" he growled as our dorsal fin got singed and our shields dropped to a heart-stopping twenty-five percent. "They're slaughtering us!"

Ambrek's evasive maneuvers were incredible for one who never sat in a cockpit before, but still no match for Nurtic and his sharp-shooting surface-rider.

"Fire, now!" Ambrek cried.

"B–but, Nurtic Leavesleft's the pilot!" I sputtered.

"What difference does it make, who's trying to kill us? He's trying to *kill us!*"

"Nurtic's my friend!"

Ambrek exhaled, loudly. "And, Crimson was my sister. *You* don't tell *me* how war works!"

Another hit. Our shields were at seven percent.

"SCARLET, FIRE AT THEM NOW! THIS IS AN ORDER!"

It was as if my military-trained hands operated autonomously at the sound of those words. Without thinking, I found myself centering my crosshairs and slamming the emerald-green button. I watched in horror as Nurtic's crystalline turned to light and debris pounded our windshield. I could only see where one of the divers got flung. We were much further northwest than the rest of the action, now; there were no other Ichthyothians around to rescue him.

"Ambrek, let's save him!"

"What?"

"The diver! Quick, before he collides with the reef!"

"Scarlet, the crystal—"

"No time to waste! GO!"

Sighing, Ambrek swooped toward him and unlocked the double doors. I opened up the shaft and, for the first time in five months, dove into the sea. At once, I was overcome by a shocking, icy rush and intense water pressure. Oh, Tincture. System's diving suits really were a sad imitation of the arrhythmic Ichthyothian ones.

At last, I caught the diver's long, lanky figure in my arms. I struggled to tow his heavy body back to our fighter. He and I tumbled awkwardly through the double-doors and hit the floor with a smack.

"Please be alive, please be alive," I panted as I undid the four latches on the back of the diver's collar, pressed the release button and yanked off his helmet...revealing a familiar, tanned face and mop of sandy, dark-blonde hair.

It was Nurtic.

"Oh, it *is* him! Oh, Tincture, please let him be alive!"

I wrenched off my gloves, put my hand over his nose and mouth and felt little, hot puffs. Relief swept over me. He was breathing!

Ambrek looked over his shoulder. "He's unconscious," he stated the obvious in an uncharacteristically-disgruntled tone. "He'll be fine. Come on, Scarlet, we need to find the crystal. Again."

Ignoring Ambrek, I checked Nurtic's pulse and vital signs to make sure he was really okay. That's when I noticed his rank bands.

"Nurtic's the Commander?" I breathed. "What happened to Inexor?" First, Cease was gone and now Inexor, too? What was happening to the Diving Fleet?

"Scarlet, we need to hurry. Your friend is fine!"

I stood. "Where did the other one go?"

"What?"

"The other diver, the one who was surface-riding. Where is he?"

"I saw him hit the seafloor before you returned with him." He jerked his thumb at Nurtic.

I was silent. I was no longer a soldier in the Ichthyo-Conflagrian War and yet I still managed to cause the death of another Ichthyothian diver. I screamed and cried in my head. It was Apha Edenta, all over again!

"I'm sorry, Scarlet," Ambrek said softly, sounding more like himself. "But, please don't beat yourself up, okay? You had no choice. You're the *only person* on Second Earth who can destroy the crystal. If you go down, so does Conflagria. Think of it that way. You weren't just defending yourself, but your country. And, theirs."

I swallowed and nodded. I could feel my face burn under my helmet.

"Come on, Red Leader." Ambrek patted the spot beside him. "Let's finish this crazy mission and go home."

I stepped over Nurtic's limp form, pulled my gloves back on and plopped into the co-pilot's seat. Though the water was cloudy, it only took me about twenty minutes to relocate the fragment. And, so, I dove, once more. When I grabbed the shard, I hoped to feel at least a photon or two…but, alas, nothing happened. Probably because the water was as cold as water could be without turning to ice. It was downright freezing. As I swam, I felt goosebumps rise all over my body. It took all the discipline I had to keep the shivers under control. Not only was my suit inadequately and unevenly heated, it didn't combat the water-pressure nearly well enough. It felt like my every bone were on the brink of spontaneous implosion. I couldn't imagine surface-riding an entire battle like this; I didn't envy the System divers one bit.

"Scarlet, lookout behind you!" Ambrek yelled.

Something hit me hard in the spine, sending my body on a wild tumble to the seafloor. I struck the coral, head-first—how it hurt! I struggled to roll over, onto my back. And, I saw the mirror-like visor of the surface-rider, inches away. He was alive.

For a fleeting moment, I was confused; it felt weird to be attacked by an Ichthyothian. I wanted to scream, 'Cut it out, you fool; it's *me!*' but, of course, I couldn't communicate with him. I was clad in a System suit, so, to him, I was an enemy.

An enemy carrying rather precious cargo.

Thankfully, he didn't seem to have his weapon. He must've lost it in the explosion. Ambrek and I didn't have sidearms ourselves; the System had to ration its tech, and seabed-scavengers weren't exactly the top of the totem-pole.

The diver kicked me viciously in the chest and my suit didn't do much to absorb the blow. He lunged for my left hand—holding the fragment—but, before he could reach it, I boosted off the reef and swam for my life.

I knew it'd take too long to open Ambrek's double-doors; the diver would catch up with me. So, instead, I snagged the half-incinerated dorsal-fin and screamed at Ambrek to get the hell out of here.

"Hold tight!" he answered, accelerating.

"Hurry!" I panted. It was a toss-up, whether I'd freeze solid or implode, first. "This suit is awful—I can't take the cold and the pressure, much longer!"

We rocketed straight up, my body pressed flat against the hull. I whimpered as I clutched the sleek fin—far slipperier than a crystalline's handlebar—with my prickly-numb right hand, left still bearing the crystal.

Lights flashed at the corner of my visor, alerting me I'd cracked my oxygen beads and was losing air fast. As if that weren't bad enough, I heard my intercom crackle, hiss and die. That's what I got for hitting the seafloor helmet-first, I supposed.

A scrape resounded from the belly of the fighter and, the next thing I knew, the Ichthyothian diver was swooping around and landing, frog-like, right in front of me. He straddled the hull with his legs and grabbed my left fist. Instead of wrenching the crystal from my grasp, he wound up pulling my whole body clean off the craft. Our helmets knocked together as he was thrown on his back, legs slipping out from under him. Entangled, we slid off the ship and tumbled into the tide.

Ambrek rocketed off into the distance.

I was stranded in the Septentrion Sea, stranded near the uninhabited peninsula of Ichthyosis in a banged-up suit with a madly-skilled diver who wanted to kill me.

Oxygen deprived, my limbs grew heavy and my sight began to narrow. The Ichthyothian kicked me in the chest yet again with his flippered foot, knocking out what little wind my lungs had left. My weakened fingers released the crystal, which the diver immediately caught. He began to swim for the shore, leaving my half-numb body behind. My eyes rolled to the back of my head…

Suddenly, a swell of spectrum overcame me, revitalizing my frozen muscles. Almost as soon as my aura crystallized, it diffused. But, that brief moment was all I needed to gain my second wind. I wasn't going to die here, floating aimlessly in the frigid sea. I was going to seize and destroy that crystal if it was the last thing I ever did. Gritting my teeth, I swam like the northwestern hemisphere depended on it.

Soon, I caught up to the diver and latched onto his back with all my might. He struggled furiously to pry me off, but, no matter what, I wouldn't relent. We were almost to the surface, now. The diver thrashed and jabbed my chin-guard clean off. Saltwater and bits of ice filled my mouth.

But, the diver gave me an idea. An idea that'd only occur to someone familiar with the mechanics of the Ichthyothian diving suits. I leaned in and bit open the four latches on the back of his collar, one by one, then pressed the helmet-release button with my tongue. And, I let go of him.

He dropped the crystal in the frantic struggle to keep his helmet on. I snatched the stone and propelled myself upward by kicking his head. I caught sight of something silver spinning in my darkening peripheral vision and figured I'd knocked his helmet off. Not that I had the time or energy to turn and make sure. Every second counted: I was in imminent danger of passing out.

I was almost out of the woods when I felt something seize my ankle. I looked down and saw the exposed face of the diver. He had dark hair, billowing in the current; a pale, sharp-featured face; and a thin, silver strip, bound across his eyes. I inhaled a large mouthful of seawater.

It was Cease Lechatelierite.

He pulled me down and struck my exposed jaw with his fist so hard, my gums bled. He grabbed my collar and dragged me like a rag-doll to the shore. He kicked off his flippers, then kicked me viciously in the gut, as I lay on my back. Struggling to stay conscious, I turned my head and spat blood over my shoulder, still clutching the crystal in my right palm.

The heater in my suit was all but useless, now. The merciless, Ichthyothian wind whipped my body. My wet, exposed jaw quivered as frostbite settled in. I could feel my skin blister… Oh, Tincture, and I exposed Cease's whole *head* to the water!

Cease pulled off his frosted visual band and towered over me, silver eyes fierce. His furious face was as white as the achromatic sky. He looked a little different than my memory of him: his thick hair was longer and shaggier and his cheeks were more sucked in.

Cease kicked me in the belly yet again and I vomited blood and stomach acid—it dribbled down my chin and splattered my suit. From somewhere, Cease unearthed a long, pointy icicle. He pinned me down with a foot to my abdomen and raised the icicle high above his head.

CEASE LECHATELIERITE

The System soldier writhed under my boot, clutching the crystal in his green-gloved hand. I held the icicle high above my head, ready to plunge it into his chest. But, a split second before I could strike, he pulled off his helmet.

Shiny, wiry, red hair fell onto her shoulders. Face thin and flushed, her laser-green eyes were wide and fearful.

It was Scarlet July.

I gasped and staggered back, releasing her from my foothold. "No," I breathed. "No!"

Here was the proof, right before my eyes, that Scarlet had indeed turned traitor. I looked down at her dark-orange suit, torn and bloodstained. My nightmares were real visions, after all.

Rage welled in my chest.

"TRAITOR!" I screamed, lunging at her with the icicle. A moment before the tip would've struck her, she rolled to the left and I hit ice.

"Cease, I-I'm not w-with the System, I'm on an undercover m-mission now, p-please believe me, please l-listen to me!" she sputtered in a high voice. "Oh, Cease, please—"

"Don't you EVER call me that again, System soldier!" I kicked her in the chest and heard the sickening crack of a rib.

She let out a terrible shriek.

"Undercover mission?" I roared. "Do I look like a fool to you? I saw you in a vision, with a System pilot, *kissing* him!"

SCARLET JULY

"Undercover mission? Do I look like a fool to you? I saw you in a vision, with a System pilot," Cease roared, "*kissing* him!"

What? Why would Cease think Ambrek was a System pilot? And, of all things to envision, why did he have to see *that?* I supposed he didn't see the part right after the kiss, when I told Ambrek I wasn't ready to move on yet because I was still in love with—

"Cease," I choked, "Ambrek i-is a Red. And, what you s-saw; it wasn't w-what it l-looked like."

"LAIR!"

Another kick—oh, how it hurt! I let go of the crystal and clutched my stomach with both hands.

My throbbing ears dully registered a mechanical hum, resounding from the shore. A fighter emerged from the waves. Ambrek, helmetless, jumped out and started running toward us. Thank Tincture!

"Ambrek, help! Help me!" I called in Conflagrian, through bubbles of blood in my throat. But, Ambrek didn't run to my aid. He dove for the crystal, beside me.

In a flash, Cease leapt over me and landed catlike on Ambrek. The two of them toppled to the ground in a tangled mess of flailing limbs.

I sat up, watching in horror as they fought. Cease was far batter trained in hand-to-hand combat than Ambrek, but Ambrek was almost a foot taller and maybe twice Cease's weight.

"STOP!" I screamed in Ichthyothian, "CEASE, AMBREK, STOP!"

Ambrek threw Cease off of him. Like a rubber ball, Cease bounced back up, somersaulting. He dealt Ambrek a kick in the skull. Ambrek staggered but remained upright. He socked Cease in the gut, then seized his tiny body, lifted him high over his head and slammed him down on the ice. Cease took the fall without so much as a flinch. He rolled onto his belly, slid between Ambrek's feet and sprung up in a twirl, like a flyer executing the spin-toss maneuver, kicking and punching Ambrek's back. Grunting, Ambrek dropped the crystal and Cease caught it. Ambrek grabbed Cease's hand with both of his and tried to pry the fragment out, but Cease didn't relent. Ambrek yanked and pulled, twisting Cease's arm into a rather unnatural position.

"Stop fighting!" I cried, scrambling to my feet. "You're on the same side of the war! STOP!"

Ambrek stared at me, amber eyes oddly captivated. He then looked down at my feet, at the icicle Cease nearly killed me with, minutes ago.

Ambrek let go of Cease and dove for the icicle. Then, he grabbed me and pressed my back to his chest with an arm across my collarbone. He held the razor-sharp tip of the icicle to my neck.

"A-ambrek?" I gasped. "Ambrek, what are you doing?"

"Hand it over, Ichthyothian, or I'll kill her!" Ambrek boomed in Ichthyothian to Cease.

"Ambrek, he's on our s-side!" I couldn't understand Ambrek's strange tactic. "He's on our side—you don't need to b-blackmail him!"

"Shut up, magic-thief!" Ambrek yelled right into my ear, still speaking Ichthyothian. "You filthy, Nordic tool!"

My brain tripped on his words. Ambrek. My co-leader in the Red Revolution. My confidant. My closest friend. The man I leaned on and trusted for five months. The man I thought I could love if I ever got over Cease. A double agent? Was the crystal influencing Ambrek's mind? No. It wasn't emitting any magic, right now. My eyes and hair felt nothing. Neither Ambrek nor I possessed even a shadow of an aura. Ambrek was acting on his own free will.

"No," I breathed. "No, Ambrek, you're not one of them, you can't be—"

"I said, SHUT UP!"

Cease's lips parted.

"Give me the crystal, now, Lechatelierite, or I'll slit the throat of this puppet of yours!" Ambrek yelled to him.

Cease looked down at the fragment in his right hand.

"Don't do it!" I called to Cease. "Don't give it to him!" The spectral web would crystallize and the System would regain its power, couldn't he see? Nothing was worth that, nothing!

Cease, chest trembling, held out his hand.

"NO!" I cried.

Ambrek grabbed the shard but didn't let go of me. He slashed my collarbone diagonally with the icicle, tearing into my suit and flesh, then dropped me like a sack of taro.

Ambrek closed his large fist around the crystal, copper and gold light shining from between his fingers. Of course—his hands were warm, as he'd been sitting inside a cockpit, up until a few minutes ago. Warm enough to squeeze a few photons out of the crystal. I felt nothing, perhaps because its emissions were weak and because my lifeline probably wasn't too twined to Ambrek's any longer. Grunting, Ambrek pocketed the stone and lunged at Cease, seizing his right arm and leg in his magic-enhanced grasp. He flicked his wrists and I heard the simultaneous snap of bones. Ambrek then threw Cease's limp form facedown, snatched up my helmet, and took off in a sprint. I heard the splash of his fighter being swallowed by the sea, and he was gone.

Cease and I lay beside one another, battered and bleeding, on the icy shore of the uninhabited seventh sector of Ichthyosis. And, Ambrek was returning to Conflagria with the rise of the System and the oppression of my people literally in his hands.

SCARLET JULY

I lay on my back as snow fell from the blinding-white, Ichthyothian sky, stinging my open wound. But, it was guilt that ravaged me far more than any physical injury. Cease was on his stomach, completely silent, only a foot or so away. Tears glazed my lashes.

"Cease," I whispered, "I'm sorry, sir."

He didn't answer. He just turned his head to look at me, cheek to the ice, metallic eyes indiscernible. I peered anxiously at the face I hadn't seen in five months, the face I never thought I'd see again. His skin was blotchy-red, like mine usually was. Because of frostbite. Because I kicked off his helmet underwater and tried to drown him.

As night quickly fell, so did the temperature. The sky adopted an eerie, navy glow that played on the sharp angles and premature lines of Cease's thin face. His silver-grey eyes looked like diamonds in the illumination, and his messy, dark hair reflected sharp strips of blue and white.

His arm and leg stuck out, at grotesque angles. A sob rose from my throat and frantic words began tumbling from my lips.

"Th-this is all my fault; I trusted Ambrek all these months—I told him everything! He knows about the alliance, he knows all the Red secrets, and now the spectral web will crystallize, all over again!"

But, there was something else sitting more heavily on my heart. Something that stirred me more than Ambrek's betrayal or Conflagria's bleak future.

Cease was still silent. But, his eyes never left my face.

"And, now, we're both going to die out here, while Ichthyosis desperately needs you, especially since the System will retake control of the spectrum!" I ranted to the sky. "Ichthyosis needs you and I took you away from them! Your death is my fault—I did it, I killed you!" Tears poured from my eyes at an astounding rate, littering my face with tiny ice crystals. "Ichthyosis needs you," I swallowed, "and, by Tincture, *I* need you!" I met Cease's stony gaze. "I never told you I loved you, did you know that? You did on August seventh, but I never answered because I was scared and stupid. Well, I'm going to say it, right now: I love you, Cease. I love you like I've never loved anyone else, not even the person I believed Ambrek to be. I may've handed the war to the System and you may never forgive me for that, but, hell, I love you anyway!"

Cease suddenly reached out and touched my lips with his fingers.

"Scarlet, please," he said, softly, "I know." He stroked my face and held my chin the way he did the day I left him. Except, this time, his skin didn't feel cold against mine, but actually…warm. At that moment, I realized I wasn't shivering anymore. Even the ice was no longer cold to my back.

Cease let go of my chin. Instead, he strained his broken body to reach for my hand, which he clasped tightly in his own. His hand was warm.

And so, my heart was at peace when I began to drift into a numb sleep. A sleep I knew wasn't really sleep.

CEASE LECHATELIERITE

Scarlet's hand was cold and limp in mine. Her large, brilliant eyes narrowed to two thin, emerald strips. Her face, usually so flushed, was pale as mine always was. Her head tipped back and a lock of her wiry, red hair flopped onto the ice.

Fear prickled my chest. Scarlet was dying. I looked down at her torn uniform. The slash across her collarbone was Ambrek's doing, but the rest of the marks, bruises and cuts were my own. I battered her before Ambrek arrived, rendering her helpless to defend herself from him. I did this to her. I didn't give her the benefit of the doubt that she begged me for. Believing she was my enemy, consumed by my own rage and jealousy, I handled her without a shred of mercy, without a hint of restraint to my brutality.

Yet, even so, she probably wasn't dying from my or Ambrek's wounds, but from hypothermia—from the frigid, Nordic environment in which no Conflagrian belonged. She wasn't dying a mage's death; she was three-thousand miles from the fiery home she loved with all her heart. The home she left me to save, five months ago today.

No one on Second Earth would mourn her death but me. She had no family, and—now that the System would regain its spectral thought-control—no friends nor allies. How ironic it was, that no one would care for the very girl who indiscriminately cherished every life on this lonely, isolationist planet. The girl who sacrificed herself for the people who exiled her. The girl who was capable of turning to me and professing her love for me, moments after I beat her and accused her of being a liar and a traitor.

All her life, Scarlet was nothing more than a flickering flame. She burned as bright as a conflagration at times, but in the end, she was as ethereal as a candle in a snowstorm.

And, she would die before me. Stranded in sector seven with a broken arm and leg, I'd still outlive her, maybe even by weeks. I'd die of starvation, not hypothermia, because my suit's heater was likely to outlast my fat reserves. And, because I was Ichthyothian—born to live on the ice.

The thought of lying here for weeks beside Scarlet's dead body, perfectly preserved by the subzero environment, was beyond unbearable. Watching her life slip away now, helpless to save her, reawakened all the grief and anguish I thought I was no longer capable of feeling. It cut me deeper than anything I'd experienced in my life.

"Scarlet," I said, voice deadened by the wind. "Scarlet!" I grabbed her stone-cold chin and shook it hard. Her frosty lashes fluttered. "Scarlet, wake up!" I knew her death was inevitable. But, I didn't want to accept it. I couldn't. "I said, wake up; that's an order!" I shook her again. "Can you hear me? Scarlet?" My throat tightened and my eyes stung. "Scarlet, don't leave me, don't do that! Not again!"

I let out a scream, clawing the ice and dragging myself closer to her. I rested my forehead against the wound of her delicate collarbone, hoping the pressure would help reduce the bleeding. Several minutes passed.

"Scarlet," I whispered, though I knew she couldn't hear anymore, "I'm sorry I ever doubted you. I love you, too."

And, with that, I cried for the first time since I was a small child, tears freezing into tiny ice crystals as they dropped to her chest.

AMBREK COPPERTUS

I stood at the edge of the stone cliff, facing scarlet-red flames that licked the golden-brown, night sky. I pulled the fragment of the Core Crystal from my pocket and held it in my fist. It was so small, barely two inches in diameter. Yet, it had the power to change the world.

"For you, Crimson Cerise," I whispered, kissing it.

And, I pitched it as hard as I could. As it disappeared into the blinding light, the cavern walls began to shake. The inferno roared in my ears. Lava erupted from the depths of the Pit, shooting into the air. At once, the fire turned cobalt-blue.

Copper and amber mist burst from the palms of my outstretched hands as the spectral web fully crystallized.

"I did it, Crimson," I yelled into the sweltering heat. "It's finished!"